"I'm going to bunk here so I can keep an eye on things…"

Lizzie was going to sleep in the stable? On the floor?

It felt wrong to leave her there, which was silly because Heath had spent many a night in the lambing barns. But this wasn't him. It was Lizzie. And when she stuck a ridiculously small pillow behind her head, he wanted to snatch it, send her to bed and say he'd watch the horse.

She gazed up at him, looking so much like the girl she'd been twelve years before. But different, too.

"It's my job, Heath." She kept her voice quiet. Matter-of-fact. And quite professional. "People don't inherit a quarter share of a ranch worth millions without putting in some time. I'll see you tomorrow."

She was right. He knew that.

But walking away from her—moving through the door into the cold spring night—was one of the toughest things he'd done in a long time.

He did it because it was the right thing to do. But he hated every minute of it.

Multipublished bestselling author
Ruth Logan Herne loves God, her country, her family, dogs, chocolate and coffee! Married to a very patient man, she lives in an old farmhouse in upstate New York and thinks possums should leave the cat food alone and snakes should always live outside. There are no exceptions to either rule! Visit Ruth at ruthloganherne.com.

Books by Ruth Logan Herne

Love Inspired

Shepherd's Crossing

Her Cowboy Reunion

Grace Haven

An Unexpected Groom
Her Unexpected Family
Their Surprise Daddy
The Lawman's Yuletide Baby
Her Secret Daughter

Kirkwood Lake

The Lawman's Second Chance
Falling for the Lawman
The Lawman's Holiday Wish
Loving the Lawman
Her Holiday Family

Visit the Author Profile page at Harlequin.com for more titles.

Her Cowboy Reunion

Ruth Logan Herne

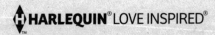

HARLEQUIN® LOVE INSPIRED®

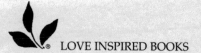 LOVE INSPIRED BOOKS

Recycling programs
for this product may
not exist in your area.

ISBN-13: 978-1-335-42823-3

Her Cowboy Reunion

Copyright © 2018 by Ruth M. Blodgett

All rights reserved. Except for use in any review, the reproduction
or utilization of this work in whole or in part in any form by any
electronic, mechanical or other means, now known or hereafter
invented, including xerography, photocopying and recording, or in
any information storage or retrieval system, is forbidden without
the written permission of the editorial office, Love Inspired Books,
195 Broadway, New York, NY 10007 U.S.A.

This is a work of fiction. Names, characters, places and incidents are
either the product of the author's imagination or are used fictitiously, and
any resemblance to actual persons, living or dead, business establishments,
events or locales is entirely coincidental.

This edition published by arrangement with Love Inspired Books.

® and TM are trademarks of Love Inspired Books, used under license.
Trademarks indicated with ® are registered in the United States Patent
and Trademark Office, the Canadian Intellectual Property Office and in
other countries.

www.Harlequin.com

Printed in U.S.A.

And above all these things put on charity,
which is the bond of perfectness.
And let the peace of God rule in your hearts,
to the which also ye are called in one body;
and be ye thankful.

—*Colossians* 3:14–15

This book is dedicated to Casey…

I was blessed to help raise you
and I'm absolutely delighted with the
wonderful young woman you've become.
You are a part of us…and always will be.
You can't get rid of me easily!!! Love you, kid.

Chapter One

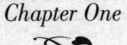

This is the chance you've been waiting for. Hoping for. Praying for. Don't blow it.

Lizzie Fitzgerald climbed out of an SUV more suited to her rich past than her impoverished present.

Her late uncle's Western Idaho ranch splayed around her like an old-fashioned wagon wheel, spreading wide from the farmhouse hub. Straight south lay sheep barns forming a huge letter *T.* The sound of sheep and dogs rose up from beyond the barns where woolly creatures dotted rolling fields like white sprinkles on a Kelly-green cake.

On her left the long, curving graveled drive wound past a copse of newly leafed trees to the two-lane country road above. Behind her was a classic Western home. Two stories, wrapped in honey-brown cedar and a porch that extended across the front and down both sides. Two swings and a variety of rockers decked the porch.

"No doubt I will spend my share of time on that porch as the weather warms," said Corrie as she stepped from the other side of the car. "What a pretty place this is, Lizzie-Beth! But I can see your attention is drawn to what brought us here." She dipped her chin toward Lizzie's right. "Your uncle's passing and his love for horses. A family trait. Or downfall," she added softly.

"It won't be this time." Lizzie strode toward the freshly built stables. "Not with someone willing to put in the effort. It wasn't horses that brought down Claremorris," she reminded Corrie, the stout African American woman who had raised Lizzie and her two sisters at the stately Kentucky horse farm. "It was greed and dishonesty. This will be different, Corrie. You'll see."

"I'll pray it different, right beside you," Corrie declared. "Then we'll see, Sugar. You explore your new place. I'm going to see if there's a restroom close by."

Lizzie walked toward the classic U-shaped stable configuration while Corrie disappeared into the house. Two equine wings stretched from opposite ends of the central barn. A row of stable doors faced the groomed square of grass that was surrounded by a hoof-friendly walking area. Six windows lined the face of the central barn, facing the equine court-yard. Curtains in the upper windows sug-gested living quarters, much like they'd had in their Kentucky stable. The whole concept was modeled after the Celtic horse farms her great-grandparents had known in Ireland. Uncle Sean might not have liked the news-paper publishing business that made the fam-ily's fortune, but he clearly appreciated their Irish roots.

A horse nickered from its stall. Another answered softly.

Then quiet stretched as if wondering about her. Testing her.

Footsteps approached across the gravel. She turned.

A cowboy strode her way, looking just as classic as the ranch around him. Tall. Broad-shouldered. Narrow-hipped. And…familiar. As if—

Lizzie pushed that thought aside. She'd loved a cowboy once, with all the sweet inten-sity of first love, but that was a dozen years and a lot of heartache past. And yet—

The cowboy drew closer.

He raised his head and looked at her, as if throwing down a challenge. And she knew why.

Heath Caufield. Her first love, with his coal-black hair and gray-blue eyes. Eyes that seemed to see right through her and found her wanting.

Her heart went slow, then sped up.

Adrenaline buzzed through her. She stared at him, and he stared right back. Then he said two simple words. "You came."

"You're here."

"I live here."

"You worked for my uncle?" None of this made any sense. Her uncle Sean hadn't had contact with Lizzie's lying, scheming father in decades. He'd purposely gone off on his own after serving in the Marines, as far from the Fitzgerald News Company as he could get. He'd spurned the newspaper empire, took his inheritance from Grandpa Ralph and gone west. And that was all she knew because that was all Corrie had ever told her. So how'd he hire Heath?

"I've been here twelve years. Been manager for three."

She flushed.

He didn't seem to notice her higher color. Or he simply ignored it. "I came here the

same time you went off to Yale to get your
fancy degree in journalism like your daddy
and grandpa. How's that working out for you,
by the way?"

He looked mad and sounded madder, as if
the demise of her family business, horse farm
and estate was somehow her fault. It wasn't,
and she didn't owe Heath any explanations.
In her book, it was the other way around, but
she'd put the past behind her years ago. She
had to. He'd be wise to do the same. "Journalism with an MBA on the side. From Whar-
ton. And enough expertise with horses and
business to handle this, I expect."

Her words and Ivy League degrees didn't
seem to impress him, but she wasn't here to
impress anyone. She was here to do a job,
a job assigned to her by her dying uncle. If
she and her sisters put in a year working the
equine side of Pine Ridge Ranch and brought
it out of the red and into the black, his estate
would be split four ways, according to the
lawyer's formal letter. Her, her two sisters,
and the current farm manager, who appeared
to be Heath Caufield.

His look went from her to the stunning
barn behind her, then back. "Twenty-eight
horses, with eight of them bred to champi-

onship lines. And you show up on your own. Where are Charlotte and Melonie?"

His attitude caused a hint of anger to fire up inside her. Should she snap back?

No. There was nothing to be achieved in that. She kept her face and her voice even. "They'll be along. They had things to finish up. And while they'll be living here, don't expect them to take on major horse work. Char just finished her veterinary degree and Melonie doesn't do well in a barn."

"She'll adjust."

The lick of anger burned a little brighter. "I believe Uncle Sean's will said that Charlotte, Melonie and I had to live here for at least a year to earn our bequests. And that we needed to focus on getting the horse breeding business up and running or sell it off. Correct?"

He held her gaze with hard eyes and nodded. Slowly.

"Trust us to disburse the jobs as we see fit. They'll do their share, but make no mistake about it, Heath." She folded her arms and braced her legs because if there was one thing she was sure about, it was her ability to run horse from every aspect of the business. "I'll be the one putting in the time in this stable. With whatever help you have available."

"Help's tight at the moment. We've got one last herd of sheep going into the hills since the government reneged on our grazing rights, and that leaves us short down here. For the next six weeks at least."

"Then we'll have to figure things out," she told him. "Because the girls won't be here for a few weeks, either." She didn't tell him why she was available at a moment's notice, how the illustrious corporation her great-grandfather began had fired her as soon as the Feds indicted her father on multiple charges of embezzlement and money laundering. No publisher in today's struggling print economy wanted their name connected to Tim Fitzgerald's misdeeds. She was guilty by association. End of story.

Not out here. Not on this ranch. Or so she'd thought until she came face-to-face with Heath again. Who'd have thought her road less traveled would lead to this?

Not her. But that was okay because she'd grown up since then, and this ranch, those beautiful horses…

This job was made for her. She knew it. She was pretty sure Heath knew it, too. And if they both stayed calm, cool and collected, maybe they could make it work. As long as they both stayed on their own side of the ranch.

* * *

She'd come.

Heath hadn't wanted her to. He'd have been fine leaving the past in the past, but now it rose up to meet him, and all because his friend and mentor's life had been cut short… with a herd of pricey horses to comb, curry, exercise and tend. And not one lick of time to do it.

Sean's cancer did this. He'd invested a crazy amount of money to begin a horse breeding enterprise, the kind of horses that required substantial bankroll, then took their own sweet time about paying it back.

Beautiful horse flesh, the kind that ranchers and rodeo riders alike loved. With Sean's death, they had no one to oversee the million-dollar industry. No one except Lizzie and her sisters, straight off a pretentious Southern horse farm that had been seized by the government. Sean had called it God's timing.

Heath considered it more like cruel fate. Either way, she was here, and if he was honest with himself, she was even more beautiful than she'd been a dozen years before. Long chestnut-toned hair, pulled back. Cinnamon eyes that almost matched the hair, and skin as fair and freckled as he remembered.

"Heath Caufield."

He turned swiftly toward an old, friendly voice. "Corrie?"

She hugged him, laughed, then hugged him again as Lizzie began to retrieve bags from their vehicle.

"You came all the way up here? I can't believe this."

"Did you think I'd send any one of my babies on alone?" She stared at him as if aghast. "Not on your life! My girls will begin this new adventure with me by their sides. Caring for horses does not come easy and it's a night-and-day enterprise. But that's something you already know."

He sure did. He'd spent seven years working their grandfather's horse farm before he'd been banished.

Corrie offered him a frank look, a look that made him wonder how much she knew. And then it was gone. "Do you expect there's room in the kitchen for one more? I don't want to step on any toes."

"There aren't any paid positions open right now, Corrie." He didn't want to say money was tight on a ranch valued in the millions of dollars. But it was.

She shrugged. "I put some money by over the years, and followed some investing advice. Money's not what I'm after. A roof over our heads, and food to eat—that's not a bad day, is it? I'm not handy with horses, but I'd like to learn my way around sheep. Such docile creatures. And the lambs, so small, like a painting from the Good Book." She indicated the size of a newborn lamb with her hands. "And of course, I am good in the garden. Always was, and fresh-grown food is a blessing." She gave him a quiet scan. "You look good, Heath. Older. And wiser."

"Smarter, for sure." He didn't look at Liz. He didn't have to look at Liz to remember the strength and urgency of young love. How could one forget the unforgettable? He couldn't, but a smart man put it all in perspective. "Steadier."

"Steady is good." She put a hand on his arm. "You're married."

She'd dropped her gaze to his left hand where his plain gold band glimmered. "I was." A rogue cloud passed between them and the sun at that moment, chilling the spring air as it dulled the light. "She died from complications after having our little boy. Now it's me and Zeke. My son. We do all right."

Corrie did what she'd always done.

She prayed.

Right then and there, her hand on his arm,

head bowed, she whispered a prayer for him and his child.

Then she stared up at him, and he couldn't bear to see the pain in her eyes, in anyone's eyes, because he'd moved on. He had no choice because he might have lost Anna but he still had his son, Ezekiel Sean Caufield. And Zeke came first now. In everything.

Lizzie had drawn close. He wanted to avoid her, especially now, remembering the birth of his son. His wife had risked her life and lost, but she'd been willing to go the distance for their child.

That set the two women a long ways apart. One who was willing to sacrifice for a child, one who couldn't be bothered.

He had no time to dwell. He had work to do and a son waiting for him. A spunky little boy, waiting to play with his dad.

He started to turn. Lizzie turned at the same moment, and there they were, face-to-face.

Anger bubbled up from somewhere so deep it should have stayed buried, but Corrie's words about his wedding ring had opened it like a fresh-dug grave.

Lizzie started to speak, then didn't.

Just as well. They had nothing to say to one another.

He reached out and hoisted two duffel-style bags, then moved toward the porch.

"Where are you going?"

"Inside?" he said, because it was fairly obvious.

She hooked a thumb toward the stable. "Who's living in the barn apartment?"

"No one."

"Well, there is now." She grabbed a rolling bag by the handle. "Leave the right-hand duffel here, please, but go ahead and take Corrie's into the house. First rule of horse is to have someone close by that knows how to rule the horse."

"You're going to live in a barn?" He looked back at Corrie. She remained quiet, just out of the way, watching their back-and-forth.

"At least until I get a feel for the place." She kept walking toward the barn. "Is it furnished?"

It wasn't because Sean had cared for the horses until he got too sick, and he'd lived in the house. "No."

"Wi-Fi?"

Sean had the equine offices built on the first floor purposely, facing the pasture. If he was throwing down a major equine business deal, he didn't want the walk back to the house to interrupt. The vision of pricey mares and geldings in the rich, green grass added enticement to the deal. "Yes. There's a full office set up with all the records. Hard copy and online. I can show you all that."

"Corrie, I'll see you once you're settled." Liz motioned toward the house. "The sooner I get set up, the quicker I can grab some furniture off Craigslist."

Used furniture?

Living in the barn? Was she serious?

One look at her face confirmed that she was. Maybe he'd been wrong. Maybe she understood the stakes. Maybe she had what it would take to help make things right.

He hauled Corrie's things inside and up the main stairs. He set the duffel inside the first room, then repeated the trip with the smaller bags and boxes.

His phone rang as he backed out of Corrie's room. The name of a well-known Pacific Northwest grocery retailer flashed. He took the call, and by the time he'd finished a deal for four hundred fresh market lambs for wedding season, nearly a quarter hour had passed. That meant he'd left Lizzie to do all her own lifting and carrying.

He hurried back outside because no matter how rough their past had been, he wasn't normally a jerk. At least he hoped he wasn't, but with Pine Ridge teetering on the brink, he might be testier than normal. It wasn't fair to lay that at her door, but there wouldn't be time to sugarcoat things, either.

Lizzie wasn't in his line of sight when he stepped outside. He started for the nearest stairs at the same time he heard his five-year-old son sigh out loud as he gazed out through the square, wooden spindles. "You're so beautiful."

Heath turned in the direction his son was facing and swallowed hard, because Zeke was one hundred percent correct. Standing on the graveled yard below, Lizzie Fitzgerald was absolutely, positively drop-dead gorgeous in an all-American girl kind of way. That thick, long hair framed a heart-shaped face. A face he'd loved once, but he'd been young and headstrong then. Somewhere along the way, he'd grown up.

"You're quite handsome yourself." Lizzie smiled up at Zeke, and despite Heath's warnings about strangers, Zeke grinned back, then raced down the broad side steps.

"Are you staying here?" He slid to a quick stop in front of Lizzie. There was no curtailing his excitement. "My dad said we've got people who are coming here to stay, so that must be you. Right?"

"Correct." She didn't look at Heath and wonder about his dark-skinned son, and he gave her reluctant points for that. Zeke's skin was a gift from his African American mother, but his gray-blue eyes were Caufield, through and through.

Lizzie squatted to Zeke's level and held his attention with a pretty smile. "My name's Lizzie. My friend Corrie and I are living on the ranch with you. I hope that's all right."

"Do you snore?"

She paused as if considering the question. "Not to my knowledge. But then, I'm asleep, so how would I know?"

"I do not snore," declared Zeke. He shoved his hands into two little pockets, total cowboy. "But I have bad dreams sometimes and then Dad lets me come sleep with him."

"I'm glad he does."

"I know. Me, too."

Heath came down the stairs. Zeke smiled his way. "This is the first girl visitor we've ever had, Dad!"

Lizzie raised her gaze to Heath's. He thought she'd tease him, or play off the boy's bold statement. There hadn't ever been a woman visitor to the ranch house, except for the shepherds' wives.

She didn't tease. Sympathy marked her expression, and the kindness in her eyes made his chest hurt.

Maybe she'd grown up, too.

Maybe she could handle life better now. That was all well and good, but he'd lost something a dozen years before. A part of his heart and a chunk of his soul had fallen by the wayside when she chose school over their unborn child.

Guilt hit him, because he was four years older than Lizzie, and it took two to create a child. He'd let them both down back then, and the consequences of their actions haunted him still.

"You've got your daddy's eyes. And the look of him in some ways."

"And his mother."

He didn't mean the words to come out curtly, but they did and there was no snatching them back. Lizzie stayed still, gazing down, then seemed to collect herself. "That's the way of things, of course."

"Do you look like *your* mother?" Zeke asked as Lizzie stood up.

"I don't. I look more like my dad and my Uncle Sean. My two sisters look like my mother."

"Mister Sean was your uncle?" That fact surprised Zeke. "So we're almost like family!"

"Or at least very good friends." She smiled down at him. "I think I'd like to be your friend, Zeke Caufield."

"And I will like being your friend, too, Miss Lizzie!"

"Just Lizzie," she told him. She reached out and palmed his head. No fancy nail polish gilded her nails. And from the looks of them, she still bit them when she got nervous. Was the move to the ranch making her nervous? Or was it him?

"But Dad says I'm asposed to call people stuff like that," Zeke explained in a matter-of-fact voice. "To be polite."

"I think if you say my name politely, then it is polite. Isn't it?"

"Yes!"

She looked at Heath then.

He tried to read her expression, but failed. What was she feeling, seeing his son? Did her mind go back to their past, like his did? Would this old ache ever come to some kind of peace between them? How could it?

"Dad, I'm so starving!"

"Hey, little man, lunch is ready inside." Cookie, the ranch house manager, called to Zeke through the screen door. He saw Heath's questioning look and waved toward the road. "Rosina had a doctor's appointment, remember? So Zeke is hanging with me for a few hours."

He'd forgotten that, even though he'd made a note in his phone. What kind of father was he?

"I'll see to him, boss." Cookie's deep voice offered reassurance, but it wasn't his job to watch Zeke, and keeping a five-year-old safe on a working ranch wasn't a piece of cake. "No big deal."

It wasn't a big deal to the cook because he had a good heart, but it was a huge deal to Heath. His first priority should be caring for his son, and since he'd lost his friend and mentor, Heath was pretty sure he'd fallen down on that. He'd add it to the list of necessary improvements, a list that seemed to be getting longer every day.

"Maybe I can be with you?" Zeke had started for the stairs, but he paused and looked back at Lizzie. "Like while Dad's working and Cookie's busy. I won't get in the way." He shook his head in an earnest attempt to convince her. "I like almost *never* get in the way."

Cookie bit back a laugh.

Heath didn't. He slanted his gaze down. "Miss Lizzie will be busy. You stay here with Cookie. Got it?"

Zeke peeked past him to Lizzie, then sighed. "Yes, sir."

"But for now we can have lunch together," said Lizzie as she followed Zeke up the stairs.

He couldn't stop Zeke from eating with Lizzie, and the reality of having her here was a done deal. But he could set limits when it came to Zeke. He was his father, after all.

But when Zeke aimed a grin up to Lizzie and she smiled right back down, another dose of reality hit him.

He couldn't enforce sanctions on emotions. And from the way his son was smiling up at Lizzie, then reaching for her hand…

He swallowed a sigh and headed for the barn.

Emotions and Lizzie were a whole other rodeo. One he knew too well.

Chapter Two

"Sean did something your father never seemed to understand," Corrie said softly as she and Lizzie approached the stablemaster's quarters after a quick lunch. She indicated the sprawling ranch around her and the pristine buildings, a trait for classic perfection that came straight from Lizzie's grandfather. "He worked hard and made his own success."

In sheep...and now horses. Only he was gone too soon.

Lizzie found the whole thing pretty unbelievable, even though she was a huge fan of great woolens made by pricey designers. Or had been, when she'd had money for such things.

"Liz."

Oh, be still her heart, hearing Heath's voice

call her name. She'd hoped for that long ago. Prayed for it. It had never happened, but for one swift moment she longed to turn and run to him, like she'd done long ago.

She didn't.

She tucked the momentary surprise away. She stopped moving to let him catch up, but then another cowboy came their way on horseback. He drew up, dismounted and gestured toward the western hills.

A deep furrow formed between Heath's thick, dark brows.

A long time ago she would have smoothed those furrows away. Not now. She'd learned a hard lesson back then, but one she carried with her still. Strength and independence had become her mainstay and they had gotten her this far.

He turned back toward the long drive, then whistled lightly through his teeth. She used to call that his pressure cooker release valve, when they were young and in love. But that was a long time ago, too.

"If you've got work, Heath, we can find our way around," she told him. "We'll take our own personal tour of the place."

He went all Clint Eastwood on her. He didn't blink. Didn't flinch. Didn't roll his shoulders the way John Wayne would have. But then, she wasn't exactly Maureen O'Hara, either.

Then his expression darkened. "There's a problem up top." He pointed toward a far-off pasture dotted with hundreds of recently sheared sheep. "Some folks hiked in and thought they'd set up camp. Campers mean campfires, and if you're green to these parts, you don't always understand the dangers. And even though it's still spring, we don't encourage people to camp on the ranch. I'm going to head up and explain where the camp-grounds are."

"He didn't tell them to move on?" Lizzie motioned toward the cowboy moving toward the barn.

"Jace did. They called him names and didn't believe he had the authority to evict them."

"Called him names?" Lizzie stared after the retreating cowboy before bringing her attention back to Heath. "I don't—"

"Slurs," said Corrie.

The older woman lifted her chin and Lizzie finally understood. The trespassers had spurned Jace because they doubted a black man had the authority to send them packing. "Someone called him out because he's dark-skinned? That's some crazy, foolish nerve right there. Want help moving them off?" She raised her gaze to Heath's and stood firm. "Give me a horse. One of the ranch ponies. I'm ready to ride."

"Whoa, girl." Corrie put a hand on her arm. "I appreciate your willingness to stand up for truth, justice and the American way, but how about we unpack before you get yourself shot again?"

"Again?" Heath looked shocked.

"Grazed. No biggie. Part of the job, at least the one I had back then."

"What kind of a job allows shooting at women?"

"I was overseeing the Mid-Central region, from Ohio to Indiana and all points south. A political story got too hot and I was with the investigative team when someone tried to scare them off. I got grazed by a bullet. It was long before the executive team decided that having a Fitzgerald on staff seemed imprudent while the company crashed and burned, taking a lot of people's money with it. Bad press is bad press."

"They fired you because of your father?" His brows drew together again. "Who does that kind of thing? If we all got fired because we had lousy parents, there would be a lot of us out of a job. Including me."

"Publishing is different now," said Corrie as Jace led a second mount out of the nearby barn. "It's not like it was when I started with the Fitzgeralds and I don't know that it will ever be that way again. There's not a newspaper or news media corporation that can afford to risk their image for the dwindling advertising dollars."

"I understand taking care of the bottom line. That doesn't make it right to punish someone for their parents' mistakes."

"Lots of things in life aren't fair," said Lizzie as the other cowboy mounted his horse and came their way. "We cling to our faith and hold tight to the reins."

"And trust the good Lord to look after us, same as always," added Corrie.

"Jace, this is a family friend. Cora Lee Satterly. And Sean's niece, Elizabeth Fitzgerald."

"A pleasure, ladies." He looked toward Heath. "Are we good?"

Heath nodded. "Let's go." He tipped his hat slightly toward Corrie. Just a touch to the brim. "I'll see you later. Make yourselves at home."

He said nothing to Lizzie.

She refused to let it get to her.

She'd made mistakes. So had he. But faith and a solid work ethic had pulled her firmly into the present. She'd stayed the course, gotten her education, and now was at the helm of a teetering agricultural business worth a small fortune while he ran the large sheep ranch alongside.

A horse stamped its foot, wanting attention. Another one followed suit.

She walked to the barns, determined. She'd get to know the horses, then the finances, then the horses again. One way or another she'd do right by both.

Anger formed a burr deep in Heath's chest and hadn't let loose in the two hours it took for him and Jace Middleton to ride into the hills, ask the campers to leave, then keep watch while they did.

By the time they'd packed their camp and pulled away in a huff, he was hungry, tired, annoyed and sore. There was only one prescription to cure all of that.

His son.

"I'll tend the horses." Jace took charge once they rode into the yard. "You go get Zeke."

"Thanks, Jace." He texted Cookie, and when the cook replied that Rosina had picked up Zeke an hour before, he climbed into his

Jeep and headed toward the clutch of four-room cabins between the sprawling sheep barns and the road. He pulled into Harve and Rosina Garcia's driveway. Harve had been working sheep for Sean for nearly twenty years. He and his brother Aldo had emigrated from Peru to work the sheep through the customary annual hill drives. For the local Peruvian Americans, the drive was a part of life, a tradition dating back to earlier times. Government grazing restrictions had changed things, which meant Pine Ridge had to change, too. And at no small expense, adding to current concerns.

Zeke had spotted his car from their backyard and raced his way before he came to a full stop. "Dad!"

The old knot loosened the moment Zeke jumped into his arms.

This was his reason for living, right here. This boy was his only connection to his beloved wife. And while he loved his son more than he could have ever imagined, if he'd known that Anna would be trading her life for Zeke's, Heath would have found a different way to have a family. As he held his beautiful and precocious son in his arms, that thought made him feel like a lesser man.

"Junior taught me the coolest things you've

ever seen in your life!" Excitement exploded from the boy like fireworks in a night sky. "He thinks I might be the best cowboy to ever ride the Wild Wild West someday, but he says I gotta get some boots, Dad, and I told him I've been askin' for boots for a long, long time." Two hands smooshed Heath's cheeks as Zeke leaned closer. "I told him I would ask you again, because it is so very, very important." He pushed his face right up to his father's, making his voice sound squished and slightly robotic. "Can I please have a pair of real cowboy boots like you and Harve and Junior and everybody else in the world?"

Heath let his voice get all squishy, too. "I'll think about it. Good boots are pricey, and your feet grow fast. In case you hadn't noticed." He deadpanned a look that made his little boy laugh out loud. "Let's see if you were good for Rosie, okay?"

"He's always good!" Harve's wife bustled out of the door, despite the bulk of a nearly nine-month pregnancy. "And he is such a help to me, Heath. I don't bend so well right now, and Zeke is right there to get things for me when the twins need something. And a true hand with the chickens and the pigs." She beamed down at him.

"They smell." Zeke screwed up his face as

Harve Junior joined them. "But Junior says if I want to be a cowboy, I've got to be a good helper and not worry about a little stink now and then."

"Junior's right. And he's a good hand on the ranch, so he knows what he's talking about."

"A good hand who needs to spend more time with his studies." Rosie leveled a firm look to her son. "Fewer sheep, more facts."

"A ranch hand doesn't need college, Mom."

"While that's true, a well-rounded ranch hand never stops learning," offered Heath mildly. "There's a big world out there, Junior."

"It's pretty big right here, sir." Frank admiration marked the teen's gaze as he indicated the lush valley and the starker cliffs surrounding it. "There's not too many things on the ranch I can't fix, things I learned from my dad. Those are skills I can take with me wherever I go. Or if I stay here in Shepherd's Crossing." He jutted his chin toward the rugged mountains climbing high to the west. "I like taking sheep upland, then bringing them back down. There's a sameness to it that suits me."

Except they wouldn't be doing that anymore, and the new grazing regulations were changing the face of ranching across the West. Where would that leave the hard-working shepherds who'd given up their lives in Peru to work at Pine Ridge and other sheep farms? Heath wasn't sure.

"I send you to school for that very reason," scolded Rosie lightly. "Because it is too easy for one to become entrenched in sameness. A rich mind entertains possibilities. And our town does not have much to offer these days," she reminded young Harve. "A failing community offers few opportunities to youth. A wise mother encourages her child to have roots but to also grow wings, my son."

"Dad!" Zeke drew the attention off Junior with that single word. "I think I'm *almost* big enough to come with you and the sheep up the tallest hills. I'm this many." He held up five little fingers. "And I've been practicing my riding on the fence rail over there." He pointed to the split rail fencing along a nearby pasture. "I'm getting really good!"

"Not yet, son." When Zeke scowled, Heath lifted him higher in his arms. "And that face won't get you anywhere. You need to be bigger to handle the sheep and the dogs and the horses. That's all there is to it. It will all happen in its own time."

He ignored Zeke's pout as he set the boy down and hooked a thumb toward the Jeep. "Car. Seat belt. Let's roll."

"Okay! Bye, Rosie-Posie!" The boy hugged Rosina but not too hard. "I can't wait to see the baby!"

"It is a feeling I share," Rosie assured him, laughing. "I'll see you next week, God willing. And after that?" She shrugged lightly. "Who knows?"

"I'll bring my dinosaurs!"

"And we'll create a habitat for them, a perfect spot for them to roam, beneath the old cottonwood tree."

"Okay!"

Zeke scrambled into his booster seat, adjusted his belt, then got down to the important matters of the day. "What's for supper?"

"Whatever Cookie came up with, but I thought I smelled beef and potatoes cooking."

"Stew?" Eyes wide, the boy wriggled in excitement. "I love stew, Dad! And cake. And ice cream. And sometimes hot dogs."

"A well-balanced diet is a boy's best friend," Heath teased as he drew closer to the main house again.

"And I get to have supper with our new company!" Zeke aimed a heart-melting grin at him through the rearview mirror. "That will be the most fun of all!"

From the boy's vantage point, maybe. Heath

held a different view, but that was his problem. Not Zeke's.

"You sure do." He pulled the car around to the back parking area, and climbed out. He was just about to remind Zeke about the basic rules of behavior around women…simple things, like wiping your face, washing your hands, no barreling through the house like a young elephant, and flushing the toilet, thank you very much…

But Zeke had spotted Lizzie coming their way across the square of grass. He raced toward her like a flash. "Hey! Hey!" He skidded to a stop along the dirt walk, spattering her jeans with fine brown dust. "Oops. Sorry!"

"I've been dirty before. I expect it will happen again, my friend."

That voice. The drawl. Softened by years of education, but still enough to draw a man in, which meant he'd have to watch his step because the drawl and the beautiful woman were far too familiar.

She'd bent to talk to Zeke at his level, then looked up at Heath, smiling.

The smile gut-punched him. Was that his fault? Or hers?

She turned those rusty brown eyes on him and all he wanted was to go on listening as she spoke. Meet her gaze above that pretty smile. Since those were the last things he *could* do, he put the trip down memory lane on hold.

The kitchen gong sounded, the perfect segue into something else. Anything else. Anything that didn't remind him of old losses and broken hearts. He'd made a grievous mistake by taking things too far. Yes, they'd been young. And in love.

But he should have known better.

"There's my young helper." Cookie grinned when they walked into the kitchen, and the hulking Latino's face lit up a room when he smiled. "Where you been, little fellow? Usually you're in here, pestering me for cookies we don't mention to your father when it gets this close to supper time."

"He is a bottomless pit these days," Heath acknowledged. "And you're mighty good to him, Cookie."

"We're good to each other," the cook teased. Then he spotted Lizzie coming through the door and his grin widened. "And this young woman might have come to help with horses, but she brought reinforcements which only endears her to me more." His grin indicated Lizzie had won his heart as well. "A man can deal with a whole lotta crazy on a spread like this, but some extra help in the kitchen is appreciated. And Miz Corrie mentioned something about Kentucky ribs that made me even happier," Cookie added. "We're gonna try those right soon."

"The best way to survive on a ranch is by being nice to the cook." Lizzie gave Cookie one of those utterly sincere smiles she'd practiced on Heath years before, but this time he noticed a difference in the smile. It was older. Wiser. Not jaded, and that was a surprise. But he'd be blind not to see the touch of sadness in her gaze, which made him wonder what had put it there.

She turned toward Cookie. "Do you mind if I take a plate out back? I don't want to offend, but I want to study some things while I eat."

"We like ambition in these parts," the cook assured her. "Miz Corrie told me the same thing. And don't you be worrying about cooking for yourself in those empty rooms." He pointed a fork toward the premier horse stables. "You grab food here as needed. It don't much matter where you lay your head, the food bag's on for all."

"Thank you." Sincerity marked her voice and her gaze. "Corrie and I will appreciate that a lot. I'll go get her now." She went up the front stairs just before Jace and four other hungry stockmen strode in.

"Hey, guys!" Zeke high-fived each one, walking down the row of men with a mighty cute swagger.

"You goin' to the front of the line, little man?" asked Ben, one of the older hands. "No one here minds if you do."

"Naw." Zeke faced him, chin up. "Front of the line's for workers. My dad told me that."

"Your dad's a good man. I respect that." Ben shifted his attention to Heath. "You know I'll take your place and guide that last group into the northwest hills. I've got enough gumption in me yet."

One of the younger cowboys snort-laughed, making them all grin, but Heath focused on the older man. "It's not that you can't do it, Ben. It's that I should."

"Ain't no law sayin' that, Heath," Ben reminded him. "Things changed back in March."

March was when they'd scattered the ashes of Sean Fitzgerald across the land he'd nurtured and loved for over three decades.

"And you should be here, keeping watch. There's a lot at stake with that next clutch of sheep ready to drop. We've got to pick our battles. If we need to divide and conquer when the odds are against us, then that's what we do."

Heath started to reply as Corrie and Lizzie came down the stairs. He paused because the sight of two women in the main house lassoed the men's collective attention, and Heath was pretty sure they wouldn't hear a word he said until the shock wore off. "Guys, this is Sean's niece, Elizabeth Fitzgerald. She's here to take over the equine operation."

Two of the men looked from him to Lizzie and back, surprised. Jace gave a nod of approval, Wick snapped his fingers the way old guys do, and Ben Fister moved forward. "You've got the look of your uncle about you, lass."

His term inspired Lizzie's smile. "My grandfather called me that. My mother's father," she added. "Not the Fitzgerald side."

Heath knew that first-hand.

Ian Fitzgerald had never been good with children. He'd expected blue-ribbon equestrianship and top-notch grades from the girls. Other than that, the man had barely acknowledged his granddaughters during Heath's years at Claremorris. He hadn't thought much of it then. The older man was bent on building an empire, and did just that, and Heath had been a little awestruck by him.

Now Heath was a father. He saw things differently, which might be why the current state of the ranch hit him hard. He wanted Pine Ridge to succeed, and he appreciated Sean's bequest, but everything had changed at the worst possible time... Could he be the father he needed to be and keep the ranch in the black when they were short on help?

"I knew Ralph Crawford, back in the day." Appreciation marked Ben's voice. "Before Sean moved north. He was a good man that never let the thought of money go to his head. A rare breed. Sean might have gotten his business savvy from Ian but his heart was all Crawford."

"Not a bad combination," said Corrie, and Heath put a hand on her shoulder.

"And this is a family friend, Cora Lee Satterly."

"I'm Wick." The man leaned forward and shook hands with both women. "Wick Williams, that is. I knowed Sean from the get-go, when he just got here and put money down on a chunk of land before anyone thought too much of it. He done all right for himself in these hills, ladies. I hope you will, too. And I'd like to say I'm sorry for your loss even though not much was said back and forth through the years."

"To have built up such an amazing business with sheep is surprising, isn't it?" Corrie asked. "It seems Sean was in the right place at the right time and everything fell into place."

"Well, it weren't sheep that built his fortune, but he liked to say that shepherding was good for the soul," Ben told her.

"If not sheep, then what?" Lizzie asked the question of Heath, but Ben answered.

"Technology stocks. Investments. Sean got in on Silicon Valley's ground floor back when everything we take for granted today seemed like science fiction. When Ralph passed away, Sean invested his inheritance. So the ranch was built on a foundation of stock options. Not stock. But the stock's been paying the way for a good fifteen years now. Until—" Ben shifted his gaze to the equine barns. "Which puts a lot on your plate, Lizzie Fitzgerald. Something tells me you're not as cowed by the whole notion as I thought you'd be, and I can't tell you what that does for this old heart. Welcome to Pine Ridge. It'll be mighty nice to have a couple of fine women on the ranch," he added. "We've been mostly men until now, so you're a welcome addition."

"And when her sisters arrive, we'll be four women strong," said Corrie. "Although Charlotte and Melonie aren't as ranch-savvy as our

Lizzie. But they're coming to help in whatever way they can."

Not because they wanted to. Heath knew that. They needed the ranch, or at least their financial share, as much as the ranch needed hands-on help right now. Sean's will had opened a window of opportunity when their father had shoveled millions of corporate dollars into off-shore accounts, leaving the three girls broke and in debt.

Pine Ridge would be co-owned by the four of them. Heath, Lizzie, Melonie and Charlotte, as long as the women put in a year working on the ranch. Sean had done it because he'd felt sorry for the massive change in their finances caused by their father's actions. But with the large outlay of cash for the equine start-up and the loss of government grazing lands, their solid financial foundation had been temporarily downgraded. If they blew it right now, the only option would be liquidation. And selling everything off would mean he'd failed his friend and mentor. That meant he couldn't fail.

"Four women in the house?" Ben scratched the back of his head, grinning. "That *will* be a change in these parts."

Unless they all ran screaming when they realized the hills of Idaho weren't exactly the lap of luxury they'd become accustomed to, thought Heath.

He glanced at Lizzie.

She was watching him. Studying his reactions. Reading him, and not looking all that impressed with what she saw.

"Dad! Isn't this like the best surprise ever?" Zeke grinned up at Lizzie, then Corrie. "And Miss Corrie says she knows how to make real good stuff and that maybe she can teach me like she did for Miss Lizzie, if she doesn't get in Cookie's way."

"I'll make way for cooking lessons," said the cook with a grin. "I might learn a thing or two myself, having a genteel Southern woman in the kitchen."

It wasn't the best surprise, but it was also out of Heath's hands. Ben saved him by addressing Zeke's comment. "It's a grand surprise, all right, and real nice to have family here. Brad," he said to one of the younger ranch hands, "are you going to fill your plate so the line moves along? You've got some hungry folks waitin'."

"Ladies first." The young cowboy indicated the food dishes. "My mama wouldn't take kindly to me going ahead of ladies."

"That's a kindness, for certain, and one I'm

willing to accept." Corrie moved forward. "Thank you, Brad."

Lizzie followed her.

The men took their plates outdoors. Heath was tempted to follow them, but Zeke had other ideas. "Can we eat in here, Dad? With Lizzie and her friend?"

"*Miss* Lizzie. And Miss Corrie."

Lizzie rolled her eyes, but didn't correct him. His son. His rules. And manners mattered. Sean Fitzgerald might have worked a roughed-up patch of old farmland into a celebrated ranch, but he'd always expected manners from everyone. Heath followed his example.

"We were going to eat in the stable office," Lizzie began, but when Zeke's mouth downturned, she moved toward the big table. "But I'd like to get to know you better, too, and supper is the best time for that. Don't you think?" She sat down and smiled his way.

She'd taken the seat Zeke usually used.

The boy didn't fuss. He sat down to her right as Heath took the seat at the foot of the table. Corrie sat to his left, opposite Lizzie.

And then Zeke reached for Lizzie's hand for grace. She gripped his little hand while Corrie reached out for his right hand. That left him and Lizzie unlinked.

He was absolutely, positively not going to hold Lizzie's hand.

Lizzie seemed just as reluctant, and the only thing that saved them from a full-blown standoff was his beautiful boy. Zeke squeezed Lizzie's hand and tipped that sweet face up to her. "You've got to hold Dad's hand, okay? Just while we pray," he added, as if assuring her that she could let go soon. "Like for a minute. All right?" He gazed up for affirmation, looking not only hard but impossible to resist.

Lizzie raised her hand slightly.

He raised his, just as slowly.

And then their fingers touched.

She didn't look at him.

He didn't look at her.

But his hand wrapped around hers like it had all those years ago, feeling both right and wrong. Maybe more right than wrong, and that took him by surprise.

It might have been the quickest grace he'd ever said. Anna would have scolded him. She'd believed that taking a few minutes to thank the Lord wasn't something to be rushed, but savored.

Not tonight.

Not with Lizzie's soft, long, slim fingers tucked in his, churning up memories he'd tried so hard to forget. Tried—and failed. Because all it took was the touch of her hand and that warm, sweet smile to bring it roaring back to life once more.

Chapter Three

❧

"Dad!" Zeke clapped a hand to his forehead as they finished Cookie's meal of thick, robust stew and fresh, warm bread. "Is it campfire night tonight? Remember? You promised."

"I did say that, yes. Wick cleaned out the fire pit earlier. So we're ready to go."

"Then this is like the best day ever!" Zeke turned Lizzie's way. "We couldn't have campfires when the weather was really bad." Wide eyes stressed the word *really* and his voice did the same. "But now we can!"

The last thing Lizzie wanted to do was elongate an already impossibly long day by going to the first campfire of the season, but when Zeke sent her an imploring look, she caved.

She and Corrie crossed the yard about an hour later, heading toward the warm, inviting glow of the wood fire. Corrie had brought a shawl, because the spring evening had taken a chill. "I haven't been to a campfire since you gals were in that equestrian group back in the day."

Neither had Lizzie. Heath Caufield and campfires hadn't been on her radar a dozen hours ago. Now they were. "I should be working. There's a lot to learn."

"Although there is much to be said for getting to know those we'll be working with," suggested Corrie. She pulled the woven shawl tighter as they approached the fire pit tucked on a broad graveled spot below the house.

Brad and Jace stood and relinquished their seats on the bench the moment they spotted the women. Lizzie started to wave them back. Grabbing a spot on the thick log would be fine for her, but Heath caught her eye.

He shook his head slightly.

Just that gentle warning to accept the offered gesture, so she did.

Zeke rounded the fire and came her way. "You came!"

"It was a hard invitation to resist, Zeke."

His grin was reward enough, but he made things even better by proffering a small brown paper bag. "Cookie brought stuff for s'mores, but I don't like them so he gave me cookies instead. Do you like cookies?" He was quick to include Corrie in his generosity as he held the bag open. "I didn't like grab them with my hands or anything so they're pretty clean."

"A pretty clean cookie sounds like the best offer I've had all day, Zeke." Lizzie had spent two days sitting in a car, driving cross-country, and she'd been studying the horse financial records for hours. The last thing she should do was add empty calories to her already messed-up daily fitness plan, but looking around the ranch, she figured her step tracker was about to get a serious daily workout. "Thank you."

"You're welcome!" He smiled up at her, eyes shining, as if sharing a cookie around the campfire was the best thing ever. When she bit into the broad double chocolate chip cookie, she couldn't disagree.

"You made a wonderful campfire even better, my friend." He giggled as he handed a cookie to Corrie, too. When she fussed over how good it was, the boy's grin grew wider.

Endearing. Joyous. Carefree.

A dear boy, a delightful child. Gazing at him, she wondered what their little boy would have been like. Would he have gotten her eyes? Heath's hair? Would he have had Heath's inner strength and the Fitzgerald writing skills? His grandmother's fine heart and gentle spirit?

Corrie laid a hand against her arm and pressed closer to whisper in Lizzie's ear. "You are wearing your heart all over your face, darlin'."

She couldn't help it. Not at this moment. And then Zeke patted her knee. "If you like Cookie's chocolate cookies, wait 'til you try the peanut butter ones with the most special chocolate frosting ever."

"They can't be as good as these." She made a face of doubt and the boy wriggled.

"I think they are!"

So sweet. So bright. Innocence and hope, a perfect blend. She met his gaze. "I do love chocolate the most."

"And potatoes."

Heath's voice brought her attention around. Three people sat between them, creating a good distance. Enough, she'd thought.

But it could never be enough, she realized when he lifted his eyes to hers. She read the pain in his expression. For his lost wife? For his motherless child? Or was it her presence causing that angst? "I still love potatoes. I blame my Irish heritage. They haven't come up with a potato I don't enjoy." The reply was for Heath, but she kept her attention on his son.

"My dad loves 'tatoes, too." Zeke leaned against her leg, keeping back from the fire. The boy's warmth felt good against the cooling air. "I do a little bit, but mostly I like everything."

"A boy with a healthy appetite is a wonderful thing." Corrie smiled at him. "Your daddy had a great appetite when he was younger, and look how big and strong he got. I think you'll do all right, Zeke Caufield."

"You knew my dad when he was little? Like me?"

Corrie shook her head. "Not that little, but young enough. Your dad and your grandpa worked with me a long time ago."

Heath stood quickly. He motioned to Zeke, ignoring Corrie's statement. "Bedtime."

"But I'm not even a little bit tired." Zeke braced his legs and met Heath's gaze across the fire, looking like a miniature version of the strong man facing him down. "Can I stay up with Miss Lizzie and Miss Corrie for just a little bit? Pleeease?"

Heath said nothing.

He didn't argue. He didn't get bossy. He simply met the boy's gaze. In less than half a minute, the boy trudged around the fire and thrust his hand into Heath's.

"Say good-night."

"Night, everybody." Chin down, the little cowpoke walked away. He didn't fuss and didn't fight. He obeyed his dad, as if trusting him to make the right call even though he disagreed.

It felt good, watching them. And different. Their branch of the Fitzgeralds didn't win any parenting awards. If it hadn't been for Corrie's love and dedication... Lizzie leaned over and kissed Corrie's round, brown cheek. "I love you, Corrie."

Corrie kept her gaze forward, on the fire and on Heath and his son. "I love you, too. And no matter what happens here, it is good to break away from the past, Lizzie-Beth. To forge ahead."

"An Idaho ranch wasn't exactly what I had in mind," she whispered back when a handful of bleats broke the night air. "But a stable full of horses is more of a dream come true than a punishment right now." She studied the flames for drawn-out seconds. "It's an unexpected twist in a winding road, that's for sure."

"What we've got in mind and what the good Lord's got planned don't always agree, but that's what makes life interesting. Some-times it's a collision course. Other times it's a wide, beautiful curve."

"I think our family has more experience with the collisions." A smallish log had rolled off the fire's edge. She leaned down and prod-ded it back into place. "Is that our destiny or our curse?"

"Neither," Corrie declared. "It's human foolishness. Your grandfather stepped on a lot of toes to build that publishing empire, and I've heard people say his father did that, too, before him. And then your daddy did the same, but he didn't have ambition. He wanted the world handed to him."

"And if it didn't happen, he stole."

"Good or bad, it all comes down to free will," Corrie said. "You see the beauty Sean created here. That's the side of the family you take for, Lizzie. The hard-working trait, passed down. All three of my girls can say that and be proud."

"Well, life's got a way of keeping us hum-ble, so pride's not a real big deal right now. And I've got a lot of work ahead of me in the morning. There are twenty-eight horses to learn about, I need to find a herd stallion, and I've got three emails from potential foal buyers so I need to brush up on lineage so I know what I'm talking about." She stood and straightened her shirt.

In a gesture of respect, all the men stood up as well.

Cowboy code… Respect. Honor. Honesty.

She'd loved that about Heath when they were young. His strong focus, his work ethic, the way he put the animals and others first. That sharpened the disappointment when he'd never looked back to see how she'd fared. After.

He'd gone on with his life.

She'd gone on with hers.

Now here they were, working side by side. Two goals, one ranch, and a lot at stake. More than she'd thought possible until she'd faced those stables and the cowboy running them.

"I'm going to stay a bit. Chat with the men." Corrie waved her off. "Good night, darlin' girl."

"Good night." She crossed the graveled area, moved by the rugged beauty surrounding her. She hurried inside, grabbed her camera, and came back out, snapping evening pics of the men, the campfire, and Corrie's sweet face set against a Western backdrop of hills, barns and land. She'd create a photo journal of this new path, something to share or to keep for herself. Either way, she could chronicle this new opportunity in pictures.

Then she saw him, standing alone now that Zeke was tucked into bed, braced against the top rail of a fence. Heath, in profile, backlit by a full moon, a Western cover shot if ever there was one.

She took a handful of pictures, knowing the sophisticated camera would adjust for light and distance.

Then she stood there, quiet, watching him through the camera's lens. Strong, rugged, determined, and looking so lonely and lost it made her heart ache.

She lowered the camera and moved toward the door. She didn't want him to catch her studying him. Wondering about him. But when she got to the thick oak door she turned one last time.

He'd turned, too. Their eyes met. Held.

She didn't know how to break the connection. For just a moment, she wasn't sure she wanted to.

But then she did. She'd learned a few lessons over the years. To forgive, to never hold a grudge, and to make it on her own.

She didn't hate men for letting her down. Men like her father. Her grandfather. Heath. But she wasn't foolish enough to trust one again, either. A movement outside caught her eye as she crossed to the stairs leading to her rooms. Furtive and low, something skulked outside, moving toward the pasture beyond.

Too small for a wolf. Maybe too small for a coyote, too, the creature slipped through the night, but the low profile and the stealthy manner put her on alert.

Foals could be damaged by rogue wild animals. And worried mares might have less milk for their growing babies. She couldn't afford to risk either, so she'd figure out what this was and how to handle it because she didn't need reminders about what was at stake within these barn walls.

She'd seen the spreadsheets. No sneaking creature of the night was going to ruin this for her, for the ranch or for those beautiful mares. She'd see to it.

Heath couldn't get into the busyness of lambing fast enough, if having Lizzie around messed with his head this much. There was nothing like delivering hundreds of tiny creatures to keep your mind occupied, but tonight images flooded him.

Lizzie, in the kitchen, engaging the men in conversation. Or on the porch, her long, russet hair splayed across her shoulders, smiling at his son. At the campfire, her lyrical voice and the flickering flames taking him back in time.

Heath didn't have the luxury of lingering in the past. Fatherhood required him to be fully present in today, but that reality had changed when he'd come face-to-face with Lizzie that morning.

The other reality was the massive amount of work that they'd have on their hands after Ben, Aldo and Brad headed into the hills for the last time ever.

He pushed off the rail to return to the house, and there she was, backlit by the stable lights. She stood quiet and still, with a beauty he remembered like it was yesterday. *Favor is deceitful, and beauty is vain, but a woman that feareth the Lord shall be praised...*

He used to care what the Bible said. He used to pray with his heart and soul.

Now he only went to church because he believed Zeke needed that structure, but the old verse washed over him as they locked eyes. He stood there, unable to shift his gaze while years melted away.

She broke the connection first and kept walking toward the stables.

In a weird reversal of roles, he moved toward the house. It had been different in Kentucky. She'd lived in the grand house and he'd bunked with his drunken father in the upper part of the horse barn, but he couldn't find any pleasure in the change. It felt wrong on so many levels. Lizzie Fitzgerald shouldn't be sleeping in a barn. Not now. Not ever.

And yet she was.

He cut around to the back door and slipped inside. He kicked off his shoes and moved into the bedroom he shared with his son.

Anna had made the ultimate sacrifice five and a half years before. She'd understood the dangers to herself, but refused to terminate the pregnancy. And when the resulting heart damage from the previously undiagnosed condition proved too much for her body to bear, she'd kissed him and the perfect baby boy goodbye. And then she was gone. No pain. No suffering. Just wave upon wave of immeasurable sadness.

Zeke rolled over. He brought his hand toward his mouth, an old habit from when he used to suck his thumb, but then his small brown hand relaxed against the white-cased pillow.

Heath kissed the boy's cheek. Then he went to bed, listening to the sound of his son's breathing, like balm on a wound. But when he couldn't get Lizzie's russet-toned eyes out of his mind, he realized that shrugging some things off was much harder than others.

Chapter Four

Determined. Troublemaker. Big Red. Night Shadow. Red Moon Rising.

Lizzie stared at the impressive list of stallion names, refusing to be overwhelmed.

Getting eight mares bred to top quarter horse stallions had set her uncle back a cool hundred grand. And based on their lineage, the healthy foals could pay back three times that without a single credential to their record.

That meant each one better hit the ground running, healthy and sound.

You are now responsible for a million dollars in marketable goods. She stood and faced the broad window overlooking the verdant pasture as Heath walked toward the stable the next morning. *And your goods aren't static. They're impulsive babies who run and jump and cavort. Your job is to keep them alive and unblemished.*

Her business major had prepared her for the financial scenario, but she'd assumed she'd be working with publishing spreadsheets and corporate executives, not living creatures. Despite all she knew about horses, she'd never felt less prepared in her life.

"Sticker shock?" asked Heath when he paused at the office door.

"Is it that obvious?"

"Don't get me wrong." Heath came through the door. "Sean knew what he was doing. He didn't play to lose. Ever. And his goal was to bring Saddle Up blood onto the farm one way or another, so three of those mares are bred to Saddle Up stallions. Speaking of which, this just came through the fax."

He handed her a picture of a magnificent red roan quarter horse. Red Moon Rising, with an offer of sale attached from Rising Star Ranch.

She sighed, staring. "He's gorgeous." She noted the western Nebraska ranch named in the corner of the fax. "I have a note here from Uncle Sean saying this was his top choice, and pretty sure they'd never sell. And yet—" She raised the spec sheet higher. "Here we are. How did this happen?"

"I don't know. Sean approached them over a year ago and got nowhere. Then this appears, out of the blue. Do we want him?"

The perfectly formed horse stood tall and proud, the way a stallion should. But he had a gentleness in his eye, too, an important factor on a working farm. "That's not even a question. Of course we do. But I thought we were short on money."

"Short on cash, temporarily. At least until we get things squared away with all the changes. But we're long on assets," he told her. "And since this is something Sean tried to do before he died, I think we need to follow the plan." He tapped the printed sheet in her hand. "I'm glad they decided to share. Sean could be mighty convincing when he needed to be. When it came to horses, he knew what he wanted and where to get it. I don't have the knack," he went on. "Sheep, yes. Horses, no. But Sean did. And he thought you did, too."

"Being an accomplished rider doesn't make me a breeder." She clutched the sale offer and gazed at the mares in the near pasture. "And there's no big name vet on hand to offer advice and testing like other places have. And one groomer to help me, a guy who doesn't speak horse."

"Not everyone's a whisperer, Liz."

He used to tease her about that when they were young, about her ability to work well with the horses, to understand what they wanted. Needed. "It's not whispering. It's just instinct."

"It's a gift and not everyone has it. Eric Carrington is expanding his place a little further south in the valley. He's looking at expanding his cattle breeding operation into horses. He and Sean talked about a partnership, but then—"

"Angus cattle, black and red." She pointed to the laptop computer. "His name came up in my searches. We passed his pastures on the drive in, didn't we?"

"Yes. And if you decide to cut the deal for Red Moon Rising, I'll transfer the money to the equine account. That's a mighty fine-looking horse right there. And there are three stallion stalls sitting empty at the moment. He'd pay for himself in stud fee savings in a year."

She tapped the open page with one finger, thinking, then looked up. "A part of me feels vastly unqualified to make this call."

He waited.

"The other part feels like someone just handed me the best opportunity in the world. To make my living working with horses.

Who'd have thought?" She lifted her shoulders lightly because when the bankruptcy rulings swept in, the horses, the tack, the trailers, the food…everything disappeared. And there wasn't a thing the girls could do about it.

"Then the hesitant side will tug the reins on the other side so you don't go hog wild." He glanced behind her and whistled lightly when he saw the big calendar she'd mounted on the wall. "All the auction dates for next year. You didn't waste any time."

"No time to waste if we've got foals due all summer. We want mama and baby teams to socialize together the first six months, so if I'm going to make this call, I need to get on it now."

"I'll leave you to it. Call my cell if you need anything. I'll be in the newer lambing barn up front, but I can get back here quickly." And just when she thought he was extending an olive branch, his face tightened. "Whether I like it or not, what happens in this barn can make or break thirty years of hard work and investment. And that's nothing I take lightly."

She met his gaze and kept her face flat on purpose.

She didn't punch him.

She gave herself extra points on that, because she really wanted to.

"Nor should you. Thanks for stopping by." She sat down, dropped her eyes and reached for the phone, effectively dismissing him.

He hesitated.

She didn't look up.

And then he left, heading toward the house.

She tried not to notice how good he looked as he strode away. She tried to ignore the breadth of his shoulders in that long-sleeved blue T-shirt and how easily he moved in the faded denim jeans. He wasn't wearing fancy Western boots. He walked off in well-made, waterproof farm boots, perfect for working stock animals.

As the Rising Star Farm phone began ringing, she saw Zeke rush out of the house to meet his dad. Heath scooped him up, noogied his head, then hugged him close.

An old ache nudged her heart with a feeling of loss, but then someone at Rising Star answered the phone. She brought her attention back to the present. She hauled in a breath and introduced herself to the person on the other end, and by the time she was through her day, she'd cut a deal on an impressive stallion and set up an appointment with Carrington's ranch manager to see two mares the next day.

They might not be what she was looking

for. Until she got here and met Sean's herd, she didn't know what she'd be looking for.

Now she'd had a first-hand look, and if Sean was willing to put his trust in a woman he didn't know, Heath better be all right with doing the same.

He'd said that Sean played to win. She did, too. And the only time she lost was when the outcome was taken totally out of her hands. But life went that way sometimes, and that meant you needed to straighten up, keep your chin up and pray your way through it. She'd had to do that more than once in her life, and when needed…she'd do it again.

Heath transferred farm equity funds into the equine account, and by the time he got showered and dressed for supper, the funds were out of the account. "You cut the deal with Rising Star that quickly?" he asked when Lizzie crossed the green square separating the stables a quarter hour later.

"Yes." She tipped a smile over his shoulder when Zeke spotted her and came racing their way. "I read Uncle Sean's notes on possible stallions, and he was over the moon about this one. No pun intended," she added. "If he felt that strongly about Red Moon Rising, I didn't want to take a chance they might renege on the deal. Hey, bud." She laughed when Zeke skidded to a stop and grabbed her hand. He looked up at her, she looked down at him and when they shared a smile, an old flicker of something warm and good ignited within Heath.

"They'll deliver him Thursday with all the appropriate testing and paperwork attached. He's already in the money with his foal lines, so unless something unexpected happens to him, we've got a perfect match for those next broodmares."

Zeke tugged her arm. "What is that?" he asked when she looked back down.

She made a face of question. "What is what, sweet thing?"

His smile deepened again as he tightened the grip on Lizzie's hand. "A brood thing."

"Ah." She squatted to his level, and Zeke's eyes lit up. "It's a horse who's going to have a baby. A foal. Some of the horses are pregnant and that's what we call them. Broodmares."

He clapped his other hand to his fore-head, astonished. "We're going to have baby horses?"

She nodded. "Yes."

"And more baby sheep?"

"Lots of them," Heath said.

"And we have baby kittens and sometimes

puppies and now Rosie-Posie is going to have a baby, too! Everyone is having babies, Dad! Isn't that so cool?"

He was about to say yes. But the pain in Lizzie's expression paused him, then he answered his son's question. "It is cool, Zeke. Having a baby is a wonderful thing, but we're going to be working like crazy for a while which means you're going to have to be a super good boy."

"Because Rosie-Posie will be busy with her baby."

"But Justine will be here to take care of you," Heath reminded him. "Jace's sister. Until Rosie's had time to recover."

"I don't even know her a little bit, Dad." Zeke sent him a glum look. "She's not like my friend or anything."

"You know Jace."

Zeke scrubbed a toe into the dirt.

"And you met Justine last year."

Zeke didn't look impressed. "I was little then. I don't even remember her and she might not know what I like to do."

"Can we tell her?" Lizzie directed the question straight to Zeke. "Can we tell her all your favorite things to do and eat and where you like to explore?"

"I can explore?" His brows lifted high. "For real?"

Lizzie stood and nodded. "Every little kid should explore things. Right?"

"Except every little kid isn't on a working ranch with animals and heavy equipment moving from dawn to dark, and sometimes after. So exploring is kept to a minimum unless you're with a grown-up."

Zeke didn't hear his father's warning. Or he chose to ignore it. "I can't wait to tell her we can go exploring! I'm gonna tell Miss Corrie and Cookie!" He raced into the house, leaving them alone on the graveled yard.

"His enthusiasm is contagious." Lizzie smiled after him.

"But unbridled enthusiasm can get him into trouble. And around here, trouble can mean danger, so please don't encourage him to test his boundaries. Usually he's tucked at Rosie and Harve's house with a little fenced yard and safe borders. Being here during a busy season will open up way too many temptations for him. Keeping him safe is my number one priority, Liz. He's all I've got."

She didn't raise her gaze to his. She kept it averted, then firmed her jaw. Swallowed. And only then did she look up, and when she did, it was to change the subject. "They'll be delivering Red by the end of the week. We might need help unloading. It's a long ride for a horse that's been a ranch cornerstone for six years with mares being brought to him. Not the other way around."

Images of rogue stallions running amok in the movies took control of his brain because when it came to Zeke and safety, worst-case scenarios always seemed to prevail. "Is that why they're selling him? We don't need a horse with behavior problems on the ranch, and why else would an established setup sell off a moneymaker like him?"

"Because too many of their horses are related to him now."

Of course. He didn't run into that problem with sheep because they were market animals. Animals bred for longevity and breeding operated on a whole different cycle.

"And," she went on, "they liked Uncle Sean. Everett Yost called him one of the good guys, and we're far enough north that we're no threat to their sales numbers. He made it clear that they liked the idea of a solid Quarter Horse operation up here."

Three good reasons. Just then, the dinner bell sounded. She turned toward the house and he went with her. "The rest of the horses look all right?"

It was a lame question. He knew they looked all right because he'd been doing double duty the past six weeks. "They'll be fine once they're back on a regular grooming schedule. Stable help is in short supply, I guess. Brad's a nice guy, but he's uneasy in the stable. And that's not good," she answered.

He flushed. "Help is scarce across the board right now. It will get better once full operations are down here in the valley, but having two bands of sheep in the hills cuts us down by six men. I thought hard about sending them off." He paused on the middle step and she did, too. "But we'd paid for this year's rights, we weren't prepped for that amount of hay or pasture and it ended up really being no choice."

"Then don't second-guess it."

She'd nailed it completely because that's exactly what he'd been doing.

"We can limp along for a few weeks, can't we?"

Lambing, hay production, decreased help and a shallow pool of available people as the local population moved away in search of jobs that no longer existed in Shepherd's Crossing since Boise and Sun Valley had mushroomed in size and popularity. "Don't have much choice."

"Then that's what we do. Is that steak I smell?" She breathed deep, and there was no missing the appreciation in her eyes.

"We send the shepherds off with a steak dinner and welcome them back the same way. Tradition."

"Well, that's a tradition I can get behind," she said. "I haven't had a wood-fired steak in a long time."

"Too busy to cook?" He followed her up the steps and tried not to notice how nicely she moved. The natural grace and curves he remembered so well. Too well.

She turned at the top step and he was pretty sure she read his mind. She paused, folded her arms and held his gaze tight. He expected a scolding. But she surprised him once again and kept to the topic at hand. "Reduced circumstances put steak dinners out of reach. Lawyers don't come cheap and while a lot of the fallout rained down on the publishing company, Char, Mel and I fielded our share. So yeah, the steak smells good. Real good."

She turned and walked inside, leaving him on the step.

He glanced at the horse barn, then the house as reality hit. Sean had said Tim's girls had suffered a mighty financial blow, but Fitzgerald News Company was worth millions. Billions, maybe, for all he knew. It wasn't like he paid attention to such things. Rich was rich and the rich always seemed to get richer, one way or another.

Evidently not this time, and shame on him for assuming things. And now she was camping out in an unfurnished stable apartment that held nothing but an old bed.

He used to be a nice guy. When had he gotten so angry that he forgot how to just be a nice guy? A few phone calls and not too much money could have taken care of that little apartment, but he hadn't done so. Why? To punish her? Or because he never expected her to bunk in the barn?

The kitchen gong rang again, Cookie's signal to come now or go hungry.

He went inside, feeling a little smarter and a little stupider than he'd been before, and when he saw Corrie beam a smile at Lizzie— while she held up a bite of steak—he realized the magnitude of the family financial issues.

And then he recognized something else.

Lizzie wasn't complaining. She wasn't whining or throwing her father under the bus. She was dealing with the situation as best she could and for the second time that day he wondered about her strength.

Clearly she was no longer the teen who caved in to family pressure to keep the Fitzgerald name pristine. In light of Tim Fitzgerald's total ruination, the irony hit him fully. Tim had sent his daughter off to terminate a pregnancy to protect the family reputation, and less than a dozen years later he'd shattered that reputation beyond repair.

Zeke took a seat next to Lizzie at the wide-planked farmhouse table. He peered up at her and grinned.

She grinned back, and for just a moment, he wondered if it could always be like that.

His thumb moved to the wedding ring he still wore on his left hand, a reminder of his wife's sacrifice, and when Lizzie leaned down and whispered in Zeke's ear, making him laugh... Heath's heart slowed.

It should be Anna teasing their son. She should be here, being a mom, a wife. When Lizzie reached for Zeke's hand for grace, Heath turned away, unwilling to pray.

He pretended to join in most of the time. He took the boy to church, he stood and prayed or sat and prayed, because he wanted to set a good example.

But he didn't believe. He wasn't like those

placid sheep he tended each day, following one after the other, being led along.

He was his own person. Hard work and honesty had gotten him this far. They'd get him the rest of the way.

But when Lizzie finished saying grace with his son, when she leaned down and pressed a kiss to Zeke's forehead, making him smile, Heath read the peace in her gaze, and a little part of him both wished for it and resented it at the same time.

But that was his problem. Not hers.

Chapter Five

Heath Caufield was a major problem and Lizzie wasn't sure how to fix it. The fact that her heart tipped into overdrive or slo-mo every time the man looked her way was no help at all, and she'd just determined to keep her distance when a text from him came through the next morning. There was a picture attached, of a solid, small sofa and chair, with an end table. For sale in town. Looks perfect for stable apartment. What do you think?

What was he doing? Being nice? Worth a look, she texted back. When?

Truck's running.

That made her smile, and when she looked out the window, there he was, with Zeke, standing oh-so-casual next to the running pickup truck. She waved, stuffed some cash and her phone into her pocket, and slipped her arms into her denim jacket as she walked toward the truck.

He opened the door for Zeke, then her. The little guy climbed onto his booster seat, fastened his seat belt and grinned. "I had three pancakes for breakfast," Zeke announced. He waggled three fingers to make his point. "And they were so delicious! Miss Corrie made them because Cookie had to go shopping and Miss Corrie said she'd throw on the feedbag."

She made a face at him, then lifted a brow to Heath once he took the driver's seat. "Is Corrie trying to sound Western? Because that's a little crazy."

"She did use the term feedbag. But then she laughed, so we let it go."

"Oh, man." He turned the truck toward the road as she indicated the sheep barn. "I thought you were seeing the men off this morning."

"Five thirty a.m. Hence the empty upper pastures. We'll rotate the new mothers onto the east pasture as the lambs drop. Give that one a rest."

"I can't believe I slept through it."

"It was early." Heath tapped a finger to the

center console, an old habit. "There's a spot where they cross the highway in a week, up north. We could take a ride up there to see it. They shut down traffic for a few hours and folks gather to take pictures."

"So it's really a thing here," she said, and he made a wry face.

"Less of a thing now. Fewer farms, fewer sheep, limited grazing. But Idaho hay is a rising commodity and when Sean bought land, he made sure he offset every purchase with land for hay or grazing potential. He didn't want to play the crop game. Too much risk in that for him, too weather dependent."

"A man who understood measured risk and return on investment."

"Exactly." He took a left turn into a small town. An old green painted sign used to say Shepherd's Crossing, Idaho, but a few of the letters had worn off over time.

"This is the town?" She didn't mean to sound so surprised, but she was. "Are there shops, Heath? Stores?"

"That's our church, Lizzie!" Heath shot him a look through the mirror and Zeke corrected himself. "I mean *Miss* Lizzie! That's where we go tomorrow!"

A worn stone-and-clapboard church sat tucked in a clutch of pines. It fit the setting, nestled into an alcove that allowed room for gathering outside in the grass, while a forested feel surrounded the setting. "That's a sweet church, Zeke." She shifted back toward Heath. "And is that the only church I see?"

He ground his jaw, then raised his right shoulder. "Used to be two others. And there were shops when I first got here, but even then things were slowing down. Smitty does barbering in his basement. And we've got a retired pastor at the church. He came up from Boise a bunch of years back. There's a gas station up ahead with a little store attached but I heard he's looking to sell. Or just close it up."

Empty storefronts faced each other from opposite sides of the road. A tiny post office sat proud and alive in the middle of Main Street, with a bright, fresh American flag flying atop a silver pole. The brilliant flag was the only real symbol of life along the short passage. "No deli? No food? Where does Cookie go to shop?"

"He makes the drive to Council. Or up to McCall. And he orders things online. He's not afraid to fill the freezer with food, but the fresh stuff requires trips."

"That will make Corrie's summer garden most welcome, I expect."

"Cookie will love it. Here we are." He pulled into the address he'd put into his phone. "Let's go see what we think."

A woman opened the door and let them in. Lizzie didn't hesitate when she showed them the set. "It's perfect. I'll take it."

Zeke pushed down on the cushion closest to him as if testing it out. "Can I jump on it?" He tipped a grin up to Lizzie and she made a face at him.

"Not if you want to live, darling. Jump outside. Or on a trampoline. Not on furniture. Got it?"

He high-fived her. "Got it!"

She pulled out her money to pay but Heath stopped her. "This is on the ranch, Liz. I should have done it before you got here, and I didn't. I'm sorry."

A part of her heart melted right there, but she couldn't afford to let down her guard. "I appreciate it, Heath. Thanks."

They loaded up the loveseat and chair, then the small lamp table. And when they were driving back to the ranch, Heath angled a look her way. "She'd have taken less for the furniture. But you knew that, didn't you?"

She'd suspected as much but didn't want to take advantage of the situation. "And she needed more by the looks of things, so this works for both of us. She got a fair price and I've got a super cute set for the apartment."

"How bad is the bed up there?"

"On a scale of one to ten, we're into negative figures."

"I'll order a new mattress and box spring from Boise. It'll take a few days."

"It's not like I'm going anywhere," she answered. "And that would be nice. Thank you, Heath." The too-soft mattress was already making her hips ache when she climbed out of bed in the morning.

He started to say something, then stopped. Kept driving. As he turned down the long Pine Ridge Ranch drive, he glanced her way. "Anything else you need right away? Like a kitchen table? Chairs?"

She shook her head. "I'll eat with you guys when I can. I'm not planning on doing a lot of cooking or entertaining, but having a place to sit and a decent bed will be wonderful. And a small TV, but I can order that online."

"Don't." He rounded the stable and backed the truck up to the door closest to her apartment staircase. "Sean had one in his room. I'll bring it over. We can mount it on the wall easy enough."

"That would be nice, Heath. Real nice." She faced him over the hood of the truck. She wasn't sure what inspired this kindness, but she welcomed it. "Thank you. Again."

Jace came around the corner just then. He and Heath hauled the furniture up the stairs, and only nicked the painted walls twice. When they got the three pieces settled, Heath looked around. "That's better. Isn't it?"

She nodded. And when they showed up twenty minutes later with the television and mounted it on the wall, she realized he was really trying, because the last thing he had right now was time.

"Done." He grinned at Jace. "And with no extra holes in the wall."

"That's because I'm here helping," Jace answered. "Lizzie, you should be all set. I wrote down the password and account for the ranch's channel service. If you have to update anything, you've got full access."

"Sweet." She taped the code to the kitchenette wall. "That way I don't lose it."

"Dad! Can I stay with Miss Lizzie for a little while? Just a tiny while? Like this much?" Zeke held his thumb and forefinger up to show a thin space. "I'll be so good."

"Lizzie's got horses to tend."

"But I'm letting them all out to graze, and then cleaning stalls, so he's welcome to hang out with me. He might be able to spread fresh straw when I'm done."

"You don't mind? You sure? Because he can tag along with us. That's what he usually does on Saturdays."

"I'd love the company," she replied as she exchanged grins with the boy. "I think we should get our work done, then see if Corrie's got cookies in the kitchen. Because I know she brought along some of her signature macadamia nuts in case she couldn't find them up here. And grits."

"I haven't had grits in a long, long time." Heath looked up at her, and they both knew why he hadn't had grits in a long, long time. Her heart went tight. She wondered if his did, too, but then she put a hand on Zeke's shoulder.

"You come with me, kiddo. You can hang in the main hall while I open the stalls. Okay?"

"Okay!" He looked so excited to be there. To be with her. Hang out with her. He chattered as he worked, a distinct difference from his quieter father. By the time they were done, it was well past lunchtime.

"Kid, we've skipped lunch."

"And I am so hungry," he assured her. "Like maybe starving, my Lizzie."

My Lizzie?

It made her smile and she couldn't bring herself to correct him. "Let's go rustle up some grub, cowboy."

"You talk funny!"

It probably did sound odd to the little boy, her drawl at war with an imitation Western twang. She shut the door to the center barn and crouched, just a little. "Race you to the house?"

"Yes!" He sprinted off with eggbeater legs, kicking up dust across the dirt while Lizzie pretended to be catching him.

"I'm getting closer," she called with a burst of speed. "I'm—"

"I won!" He pivoted on the top step of the porch and laughed, then jumped into her arms. "I must be superfast, my Lizzie!"

He was super in a lot of ways. Supercute, supersweet and quickly finding his way into her heart. Was that because she was transferring old emotions for new ones?

One look into Zeke's big brown eyes said no.

He was cementing his own place in her heart. She'd faced Heath with the realization that she had to harden her heart to him, but when he pulled out his secret weapon, a motherless boy...

She hugged Zeke and set him down.

She needed to keep her distance. It was hard enough to be living here with her first love. It was nearly impossible with his beautiful son.

She didn't go through the barn door when she headed back to the stables after lunch. She rounded it instead and came to a quick stop.

Last night's creature was creeping toward a stand of trees and an old shed.

Not a wolf. Nor a coyote. The surreptitious creature was a tattered dog with a matted coat. The medium-sized canine slipped along the edge of the trees with its head hanging low as if tired.

She whistled softly. "Hey, boy."

The dog whipped its head around, then hurried to the shed and out of sight.

She started to chase after it, but common sense prevailed. Instead, she nipped dog food from the sheep dog bin in the front barn and set a cache of food and water along the walk bordering the back of the barn. She'd tempt the little fellow in with food and kindness. And then, maybe…a bath.

A "notice me" type pickup truck pulled into the yard on Thursday, hauling a quad horse trailer. The coating of road dust did nothing to diminish the truck's wide wheel base and total muscle look. The driver pulled up in front of the house, stopped the truck and climbed out.

"He's here." Corrie was standing behind her in the stable barn. "Let's go meet this fellow."

"Red Moon Rising?"

Corrie winked. "I meant the cowboy. But the horse is probably good-looking, too."

Lizzie grinned and led the way. As she drew close, she didn't miss the light of appreciation in the truck driver's eyes. And she wasn't immune to the fact that he was ridiculously handsome. He strode forward and stuck out a hand. "I'm Everett Yost," he said as he gave her hand a firm but easy grip. "The younger one. They've always shortened it to 'Ev' to make the distinction between me and my dad. And you've got to be a Fitzgerald because you look like your uncle."

"Lizzie Fitzgerald." She shook his hand firmly. "A good trip, I hope?"

"Fine. We put up the one night and I don't think Red loved being penned, but when he gets a load of this…" He raked the mare-filled pasture an easy nod of approval. "He'll adjust. How long you been breeding horses, Lizzie?"

"A week," she told him.

He laughed. And then he stopped laughing when he saw she wasn't kidding. "You serious?"

"I've run horses. I grew up on a Kentucky horse farm, but we didn't talk breeding at our house around impressionable young ladies."

He laughed again, understanding.

"Riding, racing and deportment were the topics of the day, but having said that, I've done my homework."

He looked skeptical and amused.

"To get this right," she told him as she motioned to the trailer. "My uncle trusted me to do this and not mess it up. And he said if he could bring one of your stallions on board and begin there, he could die a happy man."

"Well, I'm sorry we didn't cut the deal quicker, then," said Ev. "No one realized he was that bad off, and when we did, it was too late. I met him a couple of times as he was traveling through Nebraska, checking stock. No matter where he was he'd always find a Quarter Horse farm and drop in. See what they had. How they were doing. This was a dream of his." He thrust his chin toward the equine facilities. "He said he didn't need it crazy big like some of those Texas spreads. But he wanted to grow it big enough so that the name Fitzgerald and Quarter Horse made a solid pairing."

"And the pressure mounts," Lizzie muttered under her breath as Ev unlatched the door. He moved inside, murmuring to the big roan horse, and when he came out backwards, with a lead in his hand, Lizzie took in a deep breath and held it.

"You approve." Ev smiled when he saw her face. "He's a beauty, isn't he?"

"Way beyond that," she answered. "Shall we introduce him to the ladies one by one? Or just walk him into the pasture?"

"He's been with a herd all his life. He'd think it strange to be separated."

"Then let's go." She took the lead and led the way to the first gate. She paused the horse, moved forward and drew the gate open.

He didn't rush the gate. He waited like the gentleman he was, and when she walked him inside, he seemed to take in his surroundings with slow, long looks. Then he entered the pasture with strong, full steps, tossed his mane, flicked his tail and stomped his right hoof twice.

And the ladies all turned his way.

"Oh, man. He's an attention seeker." Lizzie watched as the big horse stood fairly still while the mares came toward him. "And he got their attention, all right."

"You'll want to keep a close eye these first days, make sure there's no seniority issues. Horses have a pecking order like most creatures, and if you've got a couple of highfalutin mares, they might challenge him for the lead. But mostly Red just takes the lead and the ladies are content to follow." He winked at her, then grinned, and she couldn't help but laugh back.

"So. This is Red Moon Rising."

Heath's deep voice surprised her. She turned as he crossed the last few feet to reach them. "It is. Heath Caufield, ranch manager, this is Ev Yost. The younger one," she added with a smile.

Everett extended his hand.

Heath didn't hesitate. He took the other man's hand in a quick handshake, but then released it quickly. Too quickly. As if dismissing him.

"Ev, you've got to be hungry," said Lizzie. "It's past lunchtime. Come on in and we'll grab something. I'd like to hear more about Red. His likes and dislikes, his habits. I read all the stuff you guys have online and what your father sent along, but I don't want to make any stupid novice mistakes."

"Food and conversation sounds perfect, Lizzie. And fresh coffee would round things off. My to-go cup was fresh six hours ago, but I didn't want to extend Red's trip any longer than I had to."

"That stop-and-go stuff can be hard on trailered stock. Corrie, can you keep an eye on Red for a little bit? Or would you rather take Everett inside for food and I'll watch the horses?"

"I've got my phone." Corrie patted her pocket. "If there's a problem, I'll call right off. But he seems like a gentle giant."

"He is," said Everett. "My dad and I hand-raised him from birth, so giving him up was not an easy decision. But we've got two up-and-coming stallions with distinct genetics and we need to mix things up a little."

"Figuring out broad-based genetics versus the strength of family ties is a breeder's trick."

"You have been studying." He laughed down at her. "Well done."

If she thought Heath's jaw couldn't grow tighter, she was wrong. She moved toward the house, then turned. "Heath. Are you coming in?"

"Work to do," he said curtly.

"All right." She kept moving. Everett fell into step beside her.

"You guys have a big undertaking here. I checked the online stats. The sheep numbers alone would keep a man up at night."

"My uncle may have bitten off more than we can chew," she answered. "But if we can ride the current wave until the shepherds are all back in the valley, I think it can work. We just don't worry about mundane things like sleep."

He laughed, reached out and pulled open the screen door for her. "I hear you. Taking this drive was my way of catching a breath. I love my family, but a day or two apart now and again isn't a bad thing."

"It makes the reunion that much better."

"Got that right." He grinned down at her, then followed her inside, letting the door ease shut behind them.

"You might want to think about losing the frown now and then. Just a suggestion, of course," Corrie noted as Heath followed Lizzie and Everett Yost's progress to the house. "The occasional smile. Conversation instead of grunts. All the things that separate us from the monkeys, Heath."

"I don't need advice. I need more ranch

hands and longer days and perfect weather for the next four weeks so the first hay gets in under cover and these lambs hit the ground healthy. It's easy to laugh when everything's going right." He thrust his jaw toward Ev Yost and Lizzie as they went up the steps. And when the Yost guy caught the door *and* Lizzie's attention right there on his porch, Heath was pretty sure the guy needed to be punched for no other reason than that Heath wanted to wail on something. A flirting cowboy fit the bill perfectly.

"Or when one is at peace with himself and the Lord. With his place in the world."

"Don't lecture me, Corrie."

She aimed a look of warning his way because nobody bossed Corrie around. Ever.

He sighed. "Sorry. I'm tired. I feel like I'm spinning in circles. And that's not your fault."

"Sometimes we spin in circles because we've misplaced our direction. When we can't see our way forward we tend to run in place."

That's how he felt, but how could he fix it? Could it be fixed?

His phone buzzed a message from Jace. "Gotta get back to the lambing shed."

"I'll keep watch here."

He didn't look at the house as he retraced

his steps to the front barn. He didn't think about Yost flirting with Lizzie. He refused to imagine her laughing with him over a slapped-together lunch. But he hoped—really hoped—that the Nebraska rancher would get on his way before supper. He was glad they'd trailered the big horse north, saving Lizzie the trip, but the jovial cowboy made Heath look too deep into his heart and soul because Heath hadn't been able to laugh like that in a long time. Something about having Lizzie here, joining in the dance of ranch chores and campfire evenings, made him wish he could.

And that felt plain disloyal to Anna.

Chapter Six

Red Moon Rising seemed quite at ease in his new surroundings, and Everett Yost climbed back into his big rig for the trip back to western Nebraska, but not before asking for Lizzie's number.

"You have it," she reminded him. "On the paperwork."

"Not the ranch number." He grinned down at her and tipped his hat, just so. "*Your* number."

"At the moment they're one and the same," she told him honestly. "Right now I'm pretty much eating, sleeping and drinking ranch stuff."

"Is it getting to you?" he asked nicely. "It can, you know."

She glanced toward the lambing shed and didn't try to mask the concern in her voice.

"No, I'm doing something I love and maybe helping this place stay special, the way my uncle wanted. Plus I'm spreading my wings in a way I never thought possible as a publishing executive. I'm pretty sure all of this happened for a reason."

"Well, then, I wish you the best, Lizzie." He slanted a sweet smile her way. "At least until Caufield gets a clue."

She hoped she didn't blush, but with her pale skin, it wasn't easy to hide. "Have a safe trip home. And thank you, Ev." She raised her hand toward the equine pasture. "You and your father."

"Will do."

He pulled away, made a wide U-turn in the barnyard and headed for the road.

He'd nailed her interest in Heath. Was she that obvious? Still deep in thought, she relieved Corrie at the stables, pulled out her phone and scrolled through her contacts. And when her sister Melonie answered, she did what she'd always done: she spilled her guts. The only thing missing was the plate of cookies or brownies they usually shared during conversations like this. She found a fun-size Snickers bar in her uncle's desk, and felt like she'd just discovered gold as she relayed the past week to Mel.

"Heath is running the ranch?" Melonie's voice arched in a true Southern drawl. "That is the very definition of impossible, Liz."

"Clearly not."

"Why didn't you tell me this last week? I could have been on the next plane."

"You had cable TV producers coming into town and I didn't want you messing up what could be influential professional contacts just to come up here and hold my hand. You'll be here soon enough. You're already taking time away from your boyfriend and your media profile to be here. It's not like the situation is about to change, Mel. You tie up your loose ends, then head north."

Mel had been working as the on-site interior decorator for Fitzgerald Publishing's popular *Hearthside Home* magazine. The final issue would be complete in the next week or so, then Mel would follow Lizzie to Idaho. But Mel longed to launch her own HGTV-type show. Taking a year off to secure her part of the ranch would thicken her pocketbook with the inheritance but thin her career profile. "A year in the mountains wasn't exactly in your plans and I didn't want to mess up your last weeks of work."

"We look out for each other. The four of us," Mel reminded her. "You. Me. Char and

Corrie. That's how it's always been. And the boyfriend downsized me two weeks ago."

"What? Charlotte and I were already picking out bridesmaid gowns behind your back. Really ugly ones, too. He dumped you? What a—"

"Dumped like a concrete block in the East River, darling, once he realized that my fortune was gone and the magazine right along with it. But don't call him names. You'll regret it later because I'm fine with it. Although I must admit I was not quite as calm and low-key when it first happened."

"I am calling him names. In my head."

Mel laughed. "Better to realize this sooner rather than later."

"Still, I'm sorry that he hurt you, Mel. Because you deserve the best."

"Ditto. So… Are you crushing on Heath? All over again?"

"No. Of course not." She knew better. They'd crashed and burned once. Once was enough. Wasn't it?

"Do you need me to tell you what a bad idea that is?"

"No, because it's not happening. Leave it, Mel. I've got this."

"Of course you do, honey," said Mel in

about as unconvinced a tone as there could be. "Why is he still single?"

"Widowed."

"Oh." Mel's voice changed completely. "Oh, gosh, Liz. I'm sorry to hear that. So what's the plan? How do we handle this? What do you need from me? And I can seriously get on a plane first thing tomorrow if it will help."

She would, too, which was why Lizzie had held off on calling. "Nope, I'm good. Just busy and tired and trying not to mess up."

"As if."

Lizzie stayed quiet. She had messed up in the past. A lot. But she'd used her faith, brains and work ethic to move on.

"Should I warn Charlotte?"

"Fill her in as needed. I didn't want to worry her while she was studying for her certification." Charlotte had been scheduled to take her veterinary licensing exam the past week. Her goal was to pass the exam and apply to the state of Idaho for a temporary right to practice for the coming year.

"I will. She's decided to skip the graduation hoopla, Lizzie."

"Why?" Charlotte had worked for over seven years to earn her veterinary degree. "She's got to do it, Mel. She deserves to have that moment and get handed her diploma. I'll talk to her."

"I wouldn't, Liz." Mel paused for several seconds before she went on. "She doesn't see the point. I told her I'd come up to Cornell for the ceremony, but she said the sooner we get to Idaho, the sooner we get out of Idaho."

"Idaho isn't that bad," she began and Mel snorted.

"Save the sales job for next January, darling, when we're in the throes of a mountain blizzard. Anyway, Char wants to skip it. It's not like there'll be proud parents cheering her on. She's ready to get on with her professional life. You can annoy her about it if you'd like, but I'm leaving it alone."

While it seemed wrong to ignore the graduation ceremonies, Lizzie understood her sister's reticence. "Mega college loans and the urge to move past this year's craziness would have tipped me the same way. I won't push. But we'll celebrate here once you've both arrived."

"Are we wrong to do this?" Mel asked. "To take on this challenge to inherit Uncle Sean's ranch when we didn't even know him? Does that seem greedy to you?"

"We weren't allowed to know him, so that's not our fault," answered Lizzie. "Considering the fallout from Daddy's choices, I'm okay with being out of the limelight for a while. And Shepherd's Crossing is definitely off the beaten path. I get to work with horses all day and manage the business side of things without too much interference from Heath, mostly because he's got lambs dropping."

"I bet they're the cutest things ever. And maybe we can develop a woolens side business linked to the ranch's sheep output. Natural fibers are all the rage right now." The marketer in Mel jumped right on board. "Idaho's the perfect spot for something like that, don't you think?"

The thought would never have occurred to Lizzie. "That's why you're the decorator and I'm in the stables. Oops, gotta go, my mare app is signaling. I'll see you in a week or two. I love you, Mel."

"Love you, too, Liz."

She hurried to the stable area, but didn't approach the laboring horse. Commotion could delay the mare's progress. She slipped into the center stable and crossed to the office just as Heath did the same thing from the opposite end. He held up his phone. "Looks like it's go time for Clampett's Girl."

"I didn't know you had the app, too."

"It made sense." He moved her way. "Are you watching from a distance?"

"As much as I'd love to cheer her on, that would be a stupid move on my part, so yes." She opened the office door and switched on the lights. She turned on the office monitors while Heath brewed coffee. When he had a cup made, he added cream and sugar and brought it to her. "That smells perfect." She breathed in the scent. Rich. Full. Real coffee, the kind she loved. "From the looks of her, this might be a while."

"Lots of coffee pods." He pulled up a chair once his coffee was made and took a seat.

"Who's in the lambing barn?"

"Wick. Jace is catching some sleep. He'll holler if he needs me."

"Or I can page you if you're needed here," she suggested, then paused. Looked at him. "You're not sure I can handle this."

He denied that quickly. "That's not why I'm here. I don't know anyone more comfortable around horses than you, Liz. It was like you were born to do this kind of thing, but while we're both good with horses, neither one of us knows a lot about breeding them. Although with other animals it generally goes smooth on its own, so I expect this will, too."

She pointed to a stack of books and printed articles. "I may have read up on a few things."

"I know." He acknowledged that with a sip of his coffee. "But I need to learn, too, and the best way to do that is to be here. I won't get in your way. And yeah, I've seen a few mares foal over the years, but there wasn't this much riding on it. So this is different."

How could she argue with that? "Okay."

He dozed off twenty minutes in. Tucked into the wide office chair, his chin dropped onto his chest and his breathing changed.

He looked...vulnerable. That wasn't a word she'd normally associate with a strong man like Heath, but it fit the moment. She watched the monitor, played solitaire on her phone, and when things began moving along two hours later, she nudged him awake. "Hey. Wake up. We're getting close."

He shot upright, frowned, then seemed to remember what he was doing. "I fell asleep?"

"A quick nap," she told him. "Needed, I expect."

He looked at his watch and groaned. "Over two hours. I shouldn't have sat down."

"Well, all you missed was some flank staring, walking and bodily functions. But now we've got a foal presenting. Let's walk down to the outer corridor in case she needs help. But make sure your phone is on vibrate. I want a quiet birth. No distractions."

"All right." She wasn't sure if he took direction from her that easily because he felt guilty about the nap or because he wanted her to feel in charge. Either option worked. They crossed to the south-facing stables and slipped down the hall where they could follow the process through their phones but be close enough to intervene if needed. Lizzie hoped it wouldn't be needed.

Thirty-seven minutes later a perfect sorrel filly was born. Wide-eyed and long-legged, the newborn horse blinked, peeking out from the clean bed of straw. "She's a pretty little thing, Liz."

"Watch the mom," Lizzie spoke softly as she moved around the foaling pen. "New moms can get protective and spook easy."

"And with a lot more force behind it than a ewe," he whispered back, but they didn't need to worry. Clampett's Girl tended her baby, took a long drink, then cleaned her foal again.

Lizzie pulled out a checklist once they

closed the stall door. "Done. I'm going to bunk here so I can keep an eye on things."

She was going to rest here? On the floor? "Won't the app wake you upstairs in the apartment?"

"I want to be close enough to check her every hour for the first few." She set her phone and propped herself in a corner outside the stall.

It felt wrong to leave her there, which was silly because he'd spent many a night in the lambing barns. But this wasn't him. It was Lizzie. And when she stuck a ridiculously small pillow behind her head, he wanted to snatch it up, send her to bed and offer to watch the horse for her.

She gazed up at him from her spot, looking so much like the girl she'd been twelve years before. But different, too. "It's my job, Heath." She kept her voice quiet. Matter-of-fact. And quite professional. "People don't inherit a quarter share of a ranch worth millions without putting in some time. I'll see you tomorrow."

She was right. He knew that.

But walking away from her, down that hall, through the door into the cold spring night, was one of the toughest things he'd done in a long time. He did it because it was the right thing to do. But he hated every minute of it.

* * *

Lizzie stirred, scowled at her phone, then closed her eyes.

She'd checked the foal twice. The first time she'd been sleeping, curled up against her mother. The next time she was nursing, and that was only thirty minutes before.

What woke her?

She didn't know. That fuzzy stray dog, maybe? She hadn't seen it in days, but something was feasting on the food dish she'd put behind the barn. She could only hope it was the stray brindle dog.

The sound came again and she recognized the noise instantly. The bleat of a sheep in trouble. Not that she had any experience with sheep before this week, but no one could survive a week on a sheep ranch and not hear the various sounds of the ewe. Happy. Playful. Sad. Worried.

And this one sounded very, very worried.

She stood, stretched and walked the length of the barn hall separating the north-and south-facing stalls. A horse was walking her way, clomping quietly along and behind the horse was a very unhappy sheep. "Aldo?"

The bronze-skinned man turned toward her voice. Across his lap were discontented twin lambs. They bawled softly to their mother and she replied in kind, only louder and with more force behind every bleat.

"What happened?"

"Somehow this one got in with the others and went into the hills. And then…" He dropped his gaze to the twins. "There were three, but we did not realize what was happening until it was too late."

"But you saved two," she reasoned, moving closer.

"It should have been all three," Aldo professed. He sounded sad, as if he'd failed. "We should have known she was nearly due, but her mark had faded and she blended herself in. Until this."

"Aldo." Heath appeared from the lambing shed. "Bring them into the near end, I've got a stall ready."

"She can't just go out into the lambing shed with the other new mothers?"

"We'll want to monitor what's happening. She's been through a lot, to take that long walk into the hills, then deliver in the cold. Lambs are hearty as a rule, but if she lost one, then conditions were rough enough to cause havoc already. She's nervous right now and I don't want her to spook the other sheep. Why were you up? Has something gone wrong with the foal?"

He probably didn't mean to sound so gruff. He was tired. She was tired. And Aldo had taken a crazy nighttime ride by the light of a nearly full moon. "I heard a sheep in trouble and came to check it out."

"I was going to call you and have you meet us with the truck when we got to the road," Aldo told them as they got nearer to the shed. "But in the end, it was just as quick to ride them in the last half mile."

"You were in the worst place for this to happen," said Heath. He reached up and withdrew a lamb, then held the little creature close to his chest. "No easy way up. No easy way down."

"That's how it hits sometimes." Aldo climbed down, then lifted the second lamb from the saddle, easing it into his arms.

"I can put your horse up for you, Aldo," said Lizzie.

The men turned, surprised.

"So you don't have to do it," she went on. "You've had a long night."

"You have a good heart, Lizzie." Aldo smiled at her, but refused her offer. "I'll take the horse back up straightaway. By the time I get there, they will have started for the next hill."

"And by hill, he might mean mountain," added Heath. "Wick dozed off about an hour back. I'll keep an eye out here. Thanks for bringing them down."

He set the first lamb into the bed of clean straw. Aldo set the second one right next to it. "Both ewes. Pretty little girls. It was a ram we lost."

The mama sheep answered the babies' plaintive calls with a sharp cry, then dodged into the stall. She circled the babies, tending to them with her tongue, then her voice.

She was worried.

The babies were worried.

And as Lizzie gazed at the tiny twin sheep, she felt pretty worried herself.

"You need sleep," Heath told her. "Unfortunately that's been in short supply tonight. They should be fine, but we'll watch for any problems."

"Perhaps tomorrow night we all shall sleep soundly." Aldo climbed back into the saddle and tipped his round-edged hat slightly. "Here is to sleep and an uneventful night. What's left of it."

Lizzie's phone buzzed just then. "Mother and baby calling, barn number three."

She started to walk away.

Heath called her name.

She turned around.

"Thanks for checking on what you heard. That's solid, Liz."

She wished his praise didn't mean a lot, but it did. No way she was about to let him know that, though. She tipped her head and offered a careless wave. "All in a day's work." Or a night's work, she thought as she re-entered the horse barn.

Stable sounds surrounded her. Horses breathing. An occasional snort. And then the sounds of Clampett's Girl caring for her new-born foal.

The mothering thing came so naturally to animals. At least it seemed to. Were humans different? Were they too smart to trust instinct and love?

She wasn't sure, but there were times when she thought so. Times when she wondered how different her life might have been if she and Heath had defied her family and run off to a justice of the peace when she was seventeen. Was it fear that had kept her from doing that? Or had she been ashamed of disappointing her father and grandfather?

She paused outside the mare's stall and peeked in. All was well. And this time when she curled up on the chilled floor to rest, nothing woke her until the morning sun rose a few hours later.

Chapter Seven

Sean's lawyer pulled up to the house about the time Heath would have liked a nap on Saturday afternoon.

Obviously the nap wasn't about to happen. Sean had decreed that Mack Grayson should go over the will with each beneficiary personally. Sean liked a personal touch as long as *he* wasn't required to do it. He made contacts because he needed them to build the ranch, but by nature he was a loner. That kept Sean away from the little town more often than not. Had he even noticed the town's steep decline over the past several years?

Possibly not.

Heath glanced back, wanting to check on the unexpected mother in the first lambing barn, but time was money for Mack and everyone else trying to eke out a living in Shepherd's Crossing. Keeping him waiting would be plain rude. "Hey, Mack."

"Heath." Mack stuck out a hand, looking every inch the cowboy he was, despite the impressive law degree. "How you holding up?"

"Fine, Mack. Just fine."

"Right." Mack sized him up. "Nothing a half day's sleep wouldn't cure. Is Elizabeth around?"

He hadn't heard anyone call Lizzie Elizabeth in a long time. "She's in the house."

"When are the others coming north?"

"Soon, I'm told." He pulled the screen door wide for Mack, then followed him in. "Melonie is finishing up her job at one of the Fitzgerald magazines and Charlotte's about to graduate from veterinary school."

"A vet on hand?" Mack's brows rose in appreciation. "Handy turn of events. Still, having a house full of women around is going to be different. You up for it?"

"Do I have a choice?"

"Nope."

"Well, then." Heath crossed to the great room. "Let's get this done."

Lizzie wasn't in the great room even though he'd texted her.

Corrie came out from the kitchen. He motioned Mack over. "Mack Grayson, this is

Corrie Satterly. She raised the Fitzgerald sisters after they lost their mother."

"I've heard only good things, Mrs. Satterly."

"Ms. Satterly," she told him firmly. "But just Corrie will do nicely." She turned back toward Heath. "Lizzie's not here?"

"Not yet." He checked the clock, then his watch. Both read the same time, making her ten minutes late.

Irritation snaked a line beneath his collar and up his neck. Maybe being late was fashionable in the publishing world. But here on the ranch, no one wasted time, especially this time of year.

He looked at Corrie. "Do you know what's keeping her?"

She headed toward the door as she answered. "She was ready half an hour ago. I'll go check."

She was ready? Then where was she? A momentary unease niggled him. What if she wasn't all right? What if something had happened? He started to cross the room just as Lizzie walked through the front door. She looked fine.

Real fine, he noted, but he wouldn't dwell on that.

He was about to lambaste her for keeping

them waiting when she pointed behind her. "The ewe, the one that delivered in the hills." She paused to catch her breath, but the worry on her face clued him in. "I went to check on her and something's wrong. Very wrong."

He hurried through the door, and down the steps with Lizzie on his heels. He barked a message to Harve over the pager and raced to the foremost barn.

He should have checked on her before. If anything happened to her, it was on him, and him alone. He ran into the barn, his mind racing through various possibilities. Lizzie followed.

Harve appeared from the other direction.

The diagnosis was clear and dangerous the moment he spotted the downed ewe. "Hypocalcemia," Heath told Harve as he knelt beside the ailing sheep.

Harve disappeared and returned quickly with a small leather case and a bottle. "You administer, I'll hold."

Within seconds Heath began the IV drip into the ewe's jugular vein while Harve held the life-giving bottle of glucose and calcium above. Once they had the fluid dripping, Heath looked up. "This is going to take a while—it's got to go in slowly. Can someone tell Mack?"

Corrie answered while Lizzie watched the ewe with grave concern. "I'll go."

Within minutes the ewe was showing signs of recovery. She blinked, then opened her eyes with a renewed interest in life. He turned to thank Liz for her intervention as Mack and Corrie came up alongside her.

"Necessary change of venue," said Mack as he withdrew an envelope of papers from his Western-styled briefcase. "If you're going to be on the ranch, what better place to get the lowdown than the barn, saving an ewe's life?"

He handed Lizzie a copy of the will, then opened his to read out loud.

And when he began reading, Heath heard the sound of Sean Fitzgerald's voice rang through the words.

"I like things my way," Mack began. "That's not always a blessing, and when I found out I wasn't going to make it through this final battle, I did some thinking. Quiet thinking and out-loud thinking, and here's where we're at. The legal mumbo-jumbo will be squared away below. Mack Grayson has assured me of that, but here's my message to all four of you: Life's short.

No matter what you've been through,

what rivers you've crossed or grass-crawling snakes you've avoided (especially the two-legged kind pretending to be family or friends) I want you to see Pine Ridge Ranch as a fresh start, a new beginning in a land wild and free and stunningly beautiful. A land a man can get lost in and a woman can call home.

I don't know if you'll love it. I want someone to love it, and if it's family, that's good. But if not, then Heath can buy you out because he's the closest thing I've got to a son. He knows the sheep. He knows my heart.

Lizzie, I don't know you or your sisters, but I know horses and Heath says you do, too. I started something I'm not going to finish. I hate that. A marine doesn't start something and leave it go. We work, plan, strive and wrap up a mission. Every time. But not this time, and I'm leaving it to you to either make it work or sell it off. The good Lord has his own timing. My life is drawing down, but you and your sisters, your lives are just beginning, and if a share of Pine Ridge helps launch you gals, well, that's a job well done.

Two tips: Don't sweat the small stuff. Life sends plenty of big worries, the small ones don't merit your time.

Second tip: Don't waste time. Seasons come and go, and it's a rhythm. You mess up the rhythm, you mess up the year.

I'm leaving the rest for Mack to handle, but I must add this: I don't know you ladies. Never had a real chance to meet you or know you, and that's a mistake I can never fix. But I can give you a piece of my dream. If it's not what you thought, well, give it back, and that's okay. But a smart woman gives things a chance and there's something about horses and lambs and shepherds and the Good Book and all that goes with it. All I can ask is that you give it your best shot, and your forgiveness for not being the uncle I should have been all along.

Sean Michael Fitzgerald

Heath forced down the lump forming beneath his Adam's apple, because Sean's message hit home, even more since Lizzie appeared on the ranch.

"She is looking much better," Harve noted

as the twin lambs bleated from the adjoining stall. Hearing them, the ewe raised her head in concern. "I'll keep an eye on her," Harve continued. "You go back to finish up. Crisis averted."

"Because of Liz." Heath stood and crossed the pen to where Lizzie was standing. "You saved her life, and possibly the lives of those two babies. If we'd waited, we might have lost her." He looked her in the eye. "Thank you."

She didn't look at him. She trained her attention on the ewe and spoke softly. "A sick mother should never be left alone. A little tender loving care goes a long way when needed."

He nodded, but she tossed him a look as she moved away. A look of regret and disappointment. In him? It sure felt like it.

Then Corrie looped her arm through Liz's like she'd done for as long as Heath remembered. "Mothers and young ones need tending, surely as the sun rises in the morning. Seeing to them has been one of the great joys of my life. And it's good to see this extends to all God's creatures, Lizzie-Beth."

Heath watched them go from his spot in the stall.

"She's kind of handy to have around, I'd say."

He'd forgotten about Mack. He slapped a hand to the nape of his neck and frowned. "She's got a way with horses and it's no secret we needed some help with that."

"Hmm." Mack left it at that as he closed up his leather bag. "I'll go over the details with Lizzie up at the house. Then I'll come back and meet with the other sisters as they arrive."

"Thanks, Mack."

"No problem."

Harve frowned at him once Mack had left. "You know I've got this and Wick's up front." He meant the foremost lambing shed.

Heath moved out of the stall as Harve stepped back in. "I'm going to have a look around. Just to see."

Harve pressed his lips tight, gaze down.

There was nothing to see at the moment, and the reason he was avoiding the house was to avoid that look. The one he'd glimpsed in Lizzie's gaze. Because maybe if he'd been a better man back then, things would be different now.

"Dad!" Zeke knew not to be loud around the sheep, but the excitement in his voice resounded through the mock whisper. "Look what happened. Come see!"

When Heath spotted a tiny white tooth in

a sealed plastic bag, he hauled Zeke up into his arms and hugged him tight.

Second-guessing the past was stupid when his present was so vitally alive—and missing a first tooth. "That's awesome, dude."

"I know! Now I have to put it under my pillow and see what happens. So the Tooth Fairy will come. Right?"

"Umm. Sure. That's what we'll do. Want me to put it in my pocket? Keep it safe for you?"

"Yes, sir!" Zeke's grin didn't just warm his heart. It owned it. "Can we go show everyone? Cookie said they'll all be so happy for me!"

For Zeke he'd do anything, even facing down those old regrets, but when they got to the house, Lizzie had gone back to the stables. When Zeke pestered to go see her, Corrie bent low. "I think she's sleeping, little man. She had a long night and she was pretty tuckered out. How about if Dad takes a picture and you can show her in the morning?"

His lower lip thrust out. "But I really wanted her to see it tonight. Before the Tooth Fairy takes it away."

"We could wait until tomorrow night to put it under your pillow," suggested Heath. "Then you can show Lizzie in the morning."

"The Tooth Fairy won't mind?" That thought made his eyes go round. "She can come tomorrow night instead?"

"Absolutely, partner."

"Then let's do that." Zeke thrust his hand into Heath's. "I don't mind waiting, Dad. Because I want Lizzie—"

Heath arched a brow.

"*Miss* Lizzie to be so happy for me, too," he corrected himself. "Because that makes everything special."

Corrie smiled. And Harve's silence in the barn punctuated the air, making him wonder why they didn't just come out and say what they were thinking.

Because you'll get defensive and overreact.

He'd been doing both for too long. But with so many plates spinning in the air, he wasn't sure how to stop. Take a breath. Be a nice guy again.

But if this many people were tiptoeing around him, he needed to wise up. And as soon as he could take a deep breath, he'd do just that.

"Liz?"

Lizzie scrunched her pillow into a tighter ball and rolled over, but the annoying voice sounded again.

"Liz? Are you awake? It's Heath."

Did he think she didn't recognize his voice? She jammed the pillow over her face for a few seconds before tossing it aside and creeping to the door. "Of course I wasn't awake," she whispered when she opened the door. "It's three-thirty in the morning. No one is awake by choice at this hour, Heath. Except you."

"Rosie is in labor," he explained. "Harve wants me to wait with him at the hospital but I need someone to watch Zeke."

"Zeke, who is sound asleep right now?" She yawned. "You woke me up to ask me to watch a sleeping child?"

"He'll be up in a few hours, and I figured it was smarter to talk to someone rather than leave a note. Listen, never mind..." He began to back away. "I can wake the little guy and take him along."

"Don't be ridiculous. Of course I'll watch him. What are you waiting for?" She motioned to the stairs. "Go keep your friends company as they welcome their child into the world." She didn't say what she was thinking, that she'd have given anything to have that kind of support from him twelve years ago.

She'd thought she'd dealt with that time of sadness. Maybe being here, with Heath, stirred a pot that had been simmering all these years.

"Thanks." He started away, then turned back. "Rosie's lost babies in the past so they're both kind of scared. More than most, I expect."

Oh, her heart.

To hear the emotion in his voice over someone else's sadness—and nothing for their own. She had to tamp down an emotional surge before she said too much. "Go."

He took the stairs quickly but quietly. The soft click of the stable door marked his exit.

She tiptoed back into the room, grabbed her laptop and slipped downstairs. She peeked into Girlie's stall.

All was well.

She crossed the chilled grass and welcomed the warmth of the big house once she got inside. She made a quick cup of coffee, then curled up in a wide-backed chair, opened her laptop and tried to crunch figures.

Despite her efforts, all she could see was Heath's focus and concentration as he labored to save a ewe's life. One ewe, out of a few thousand.

Was the ewe that important? Clearly she was.

She opened a new doc file and began again, starting with the ewe's mistaken trail ride, into the hills. And how a dedicated shepherd rode through the night to bring mother and children home. She didn't make Heath the focus. She used Aldo for that, the small, tan-skinned shepherd, putting the needs of the animals foremost.

By the time she was done, she had a solid article about a true cowboy, the kind of thing that showed the Western heart, beating true.

It read differently than her previous stories. More depth. More emotion. Was that because of the circumstance or the cowboys? Both... and maybe her, too.

The patter of footsteps came her way just before seven o'clock. "Miss Lizzie?" Zeke slid to a stop at the end of the short hall linking the front of the big house to the back wing. "Is my dad out here?"

"He's not," she replied as she set the computer aside. "He's with Rosie and Harve because they think the baby's about to be born. So Daddy asked me to keep an eye on you. Okay?"

"The baby might be born today?" His eyes went wide when he lifted two dark, little brows. His teeth flashed white in a bright grin, revealing a tiny new gap. "This might be the best day ever! First, there's this." He opened his mouth extra wide and grinned, showing off the empty front space. "I wanted to show you last night, but Dad said you needed to get some sleep."

She smiled at the boy. "He was right, so thank you both. Did you put it under your pillow?"

He shook his head, surprising her. "I wanted you to see it, and if the fairy tooked it away, you would never ever get to see it. But you can see it today and then we can put it under my pillow tonight. Okay?"

"More than okay," she assured him. "And thank you so much for thinking of me. That was really nice of you to do, Zeke-man."

"Well, Daddy and I both kinda did it."

His innocent words made her heart leap. She tamped it down quickly. "You hungry?"

He shook his head.

"Thirsty?"

"Can I have chocolate milk?"

She had no idea if Cookie kept chocolate milk on hand, but she'd seen chocolate syrup in the fridge. "Sure can."

"And maybe toast," he added. He followed her into the kitchen and pulled himself up onto one of the tall stools. She had to stop herself from cautioning him to not to fall. He handled the climb and the balance with the ease of an expert.

"Cinnamon sugar toast?"

"Yes!" He giggled. "My favorites!"

"Glad to oblige, my friend." She made the toast and used the hand-held frother to mix his chocolate milk, filling the glass with creamy bubbles. When she handed it to him, his eyes went round.

"It's like a milk shake." He whispered the words as he sipped the milk. "You should tell my dad how to make it this good, I bet he doesn't even know! You can help him!"

She wasn't sure his dad would welcome her advice, but she agreed. "I'll tell him. So what are you and I going to do today? After we check the new mama sheep, of course."

"I think we're supposed to go on a horse-back ride." He peered up at the calendar with a scrunched brow. "Do I get to stay here all day?"

"You do. Rosie won't be watching you for a while because she'll be busy with the baby."

"You can't leave babies alone," he assured her. "When I'm with Rosie-Posie, I can't do too much because she has to watch 'Lencia's babies now. They're so little and they just crawl around and mess up my toys. Even if I put the toys on the couch, they can reach them now."

"Two babies?"

He made a grumpy face and nodded.

"I bet they're cute," she went on as she brewed fresh coffee.

"They kinda smell bad sometimes, but they smile at me when I make stuff for them. Then they wreck it," he added. "But on this day it's just you and me doin' stuff." He looked up, expectant. "Like riding a horse together. That's something we could do!" Anticipation brightened his eyes.

"Do you have a helmet?"

He nodded.

"Then we're on, my friend. After breakfast. And after we check the mama sheep. Honey's Money is a good mount and they didn't take her into the hills." Honey was a placid but bright-moving ranch horse. Old enough to be trustworthy and young enough to work the milling sheep as needed.

He drew those little brows tight, as if concerned. "It's a ewe, Miss Lizzie. A mama sheep is always a ewe." His tone wasn't impertinent, but he sure sounded like he might be doubting her intelligence, so she leaned in and met him eye-to-eye.

"A ewe can still be a mama sheep. The terms can be synonymous if the sheep has had a baby. So she's a ewe..." She lifted a brow and held his gaze to make her point. "But she's also a mother or mama sheep. And where I come from, little boys don't correct their elders."

"Their what?" He frowned, surprised.

"Grown-ups. Little boys listen and learn, and they don't boss grown-ups around."

"Oh." Guilt made him cringe. "My dad says that, too."

"Your dad and I are in complete agreement. Once you're done, let's head to the barn."

He chugged his chocolate milk in seconds and grabbed the rest of his toast. "I can eat this on the way. Come on!" He grabbed her hand in his.

And held an instant part of her heart, as well.

"I love helping with the farm," he told her, skipping alongside once they cleared the steps. "I love big, huge barns and horsies and all of it. But mostly I love the sheep and the little lambs. They make me smile."

"Me, too."

He peered up, interested. "Did you have a horse when you were little, Miss Lizzie?"

She had. A big, beautiful bay mare that sensed her every move. A marvelous jumper, a sterling competitor. Gone now, like all the rest. She swallowed around a lump in her throat and nodded. "I did. Her name was Maeve and she was my special friend."

"That's a funny name for a horse."

"I suppose you think Honey's Money is normal?"

His expression said it was.

"I lived on an Irish farm and a lot of the horses had Irish names." She didn't call Claremorris home. The expansive holding hadn't been home to her in decades, but she'd missed working the horse barn. Feeding, tending, grooming, riding. She hadn't realized how much until she'd stepped into her current position, a chance that felt like home. A real home with a real job.

Zeke released her hand and raced into the barn. She started to chase after him, then realized the boy knew his way around better than she did. He paused at the right stall, stepped up on a rail, and peered in. "One happy sheep!" he announced in an excited but soft voice. "And two little lambs!"

The discontented cries of the lambs had changed to quiet bleats of satisfaction overnight. The ewe appeared better. One hundred percent improved. She watched the babies snuggle in against their mother's abundant udder as they dozed off.

Sweet contentment had replaced angst and worry.

Successful mother. Satisfied babies. The dream come true that didn't always come out that way.

"I think that baby is so happy."

Zeke's little voice broke her mental musings. "Why's that, my friend?"

"Well, she's got a mama to snuggle her." His matter-of-fact tone was belied by the longing marking his face and his gray-blue eyes. "I think my mama used to snuggle me just like that. When I was little," he added.

The hunger in his gaze softened the part of her heart she'd put on hold long ago. "I'm sure she did."

"My dad misses her sometimes." His voice turned more pragmatic again. "He gets that funny look when I talk about her, so then I don't talk about her so much. Can we ride now?"

They sure could. Anything to get out of talking about lost mothers and sad children. She'd lived the scenario, losing her mother when she was just shy of six years old, but Zeke had one big difference. His father loved him. Doted on him.

Tim Fitzgerald loved Tim Fitzgerald. He'd never pretended his girls meant much. In return, the three sisters had grown up between Corrie's loving kindness and their grandparents' somewhat aristocratic affection. It could have been so much worse, she knew, but she'd learned that wealth and status didn't replace love and that was a valuable lesson.

She helped Zeke down from the rail. "Let's get Honey ready, shall we?"

"Sure!"

She snugged the boy in front of her once the horse was saddled and headed across the adjacent field.

Rugged hills became mountains to the north and northwest. The wide valley continued beyond the ranch, in the direction of Shepherd's Crossing. As they moved uphill, she spotted other homes, other farms, sporadically spaced, and when they got to an intermediate ledge, the distant image of a town came into view. From here, she couldn't see the decay, the flaking paint, the listing shutters. From here the town offered an image of what it had been before times got hard. Small. Compact. Cozy.

The valley splayed green and lush as the spring greening moved up the hills. Flat land spread from side to side, and the curve of a creek or small river marked an almost central path with mountains to their back. The beauty of the land lay different than Kentucky and light years from Louisville.

Her phone buzzed in her pocket. She withdrew it carefully, keeping a snug hold on Zeke. No baby yet, maybe C-section. I know I shouldn't worry, but I am. Thanks for watching little man.

"Is that from my dad? Did Rosie-Posie have the baby?"

She kept the details to herself and tried to sound relaxed. "Not yet, but they think it will be soon."

Zeke turned his head. "Rosie-Posie says we can pray anywhere." His voice and expression turned serious. "It's not just for goin' to church and stuff, so maybe you and me can pray for her and for the baby and for my frog that got stepped on last week. Because I miss my froggie a lot. Okay?"

"Very okay."

She let him lead the prayer, and when he was done, he looked back up at her. "You're apposed to say 'amen'," he reminded her.

"Amen." She smiled down at him, and then, on impulse, she leaned her cheek down, against his. "God bless you, little man."

He leaned his cheek into hers, then shifted again. "Did you bring some snacks? My dad always has snacks in his bag."

She hadn't considered such a thing. "No. Sorry. But we can head back and see what Cookie's up to."

"Today is his day off."

"Corrie, then. And maybe we can do something in the kitchen together. Would you like that?" She angled the horse along the ridge edge, then down an easy grade trail. "Cookies?"

"I love cookies!"

"And I like making cookies. I've been making them since I was a little girl. Corrie taught me."

"Well, she's very smart."

Lizzie smiled, and as Zeke relaxed against her, her heart eased a little more. It felt good to hold the boy, talk with him, laugh with him.

She hadn't expected that. How natural this would seem, despite the awkwardness of the situation.

"Thank you for bringing me on a ride." Zeke sounded peaceful, clearly comfortable and wonderfully content. "It's my favorite thing, Miss Lizzie."

Having grown up on a horse farm, she understood that completely. "Mine, too." She'd longed for that kind of tranquil therapy for years. How much it had meant to saddle up Maeve and hit the ground running.

Maybe because she had been naive then.

As she hit the flats, she encouraged the horse to a gentle lope. Mane flying, Honey cantered her way across the unfenced pasture like a master. Not too fast, not too slow, enough to make Zeke laugh with delight while she held him snug with one arm.

When she slowed the horse to a cooling walk, Zeke squealed softly. "I love going so fast, Miss Lizzie. This was the best ride ever!"

She'd had a lot of sweet rides in her youth. She'd brought home many a ribbon and trophy as a young equestrian. But Zeke was right. Holding him on the saddle and letting the gentle mare fly free might have been the sweetest ride she'd ever taken.

Chapter Eight

The sight of Zeke in Lizzie's arms, curled on the couch in the great room, made Heath stop short later that afternoon.

His breath caught somewhere in the center of his chest. His heart winced, then continued beating.

She looked beautiful, holding his son, as both slept. Her lashes lay dark against her pale skin.

And Zeke's lashes lay black against more coppery tones while his brown face was tucked beneath hers.

The peaceful scene looked natural.

It wasn't.

He knew that. His son was a total blessing despite the grievous result of Anna's pregnancy. He'd been conceived in love…

His conscience gave him a sharp mental kick.

That first baby had been conceived in love, too. A younger love, fierce in its beauty and excitement. As he watched Lizzie snuggle Zeke in sweet repose, he realized a marked difference.

He'd married Anna. He'd gone about things the right way that time. He'd made her his wife in front of God and a small gathering at the Holy Grace of God Church in the village.

He'd made no such vow to Lizzie. He'd let her father and grandfather browbeat him into leaving while she'd ended the pregnancy. Anguish had begun his journey north once Sean Fitzgerald contacted him, and anger had taken over about halfway to Idaho.

And yet—

If he hadn't been strong enough to fight for the girl, was the outcome more his fault than he'd been willing to believe back then?

Lizzie's eyes opened.

His heart paused. His mind raced back, over the years. She'd been pretty back then.

She was beautiful now. She blinked slowly, saw him, and her gaze clouded. Then she seemed to remember Zeke and her arms folded around him in a protective gesture. "Is he still sleeping?" She whispered the words, stirring more old memories.

Heath nodded.

She shifted slightly and adjusted the curled-up boy as she did. When Heath reached for him, she shook her head. "Don't disturb him, he's comfortable. We had an early morning and a busy day," she went on, and Heath couldn't help but notice how she cradled the five-year-old against her chest. "I got schooled in sheep, then I schooled him in cookies, horses and chocolate milk bubbles. A good day, all in all. How is Rosina doing?"

He sat along the edge of the rugged sofa table, perfect for propping feet after a long day, or holding a mug of coffee. "They ended up doing the C-section, but the baby's safe and sound." He paused. "And tiny. I forgot how small babies really are." He let his gaze rest on Zeke for a few seconds. "Anyway, she's beautiful. Rosie's doing all right, and Harve looked shell-shocked. But happy. So happy, both of them. She'll be home in a couple of days which seems really quick for a procedure like that. But then sheep recover from C-sections pretty quickly, so maybe I'm being overprotective."

Her smile faded. She sat more upright and indicated Zeke with a glance. "On second thought, can you take him, please? I need to get back to work."

Her voice had been soft and lyrical. Now

it was clipped. "Sure." He lifted the boy to his chest. "Thanks for watching him, Liz."

"Glad to help."

Was she? It'd seemed like it, and then… not so much. He tucked Zeke into his bed, yawned, and wished he could join the little guy, but there were things to do. Sleep would have to wait.

He walked outside, hands in his pockets. Seeing Rosie in labor, then seeing baby Johanna in her father's arms, thrust him back in time. Anna had been a scheduled C-section to spare her heart the rigors of labor. She'd wakened long enough to see Zeke. To hold him. To smile at her son and bless him before he was whisked off to the NICU.

She'd lingered for three days, in and out of a semi-conscious state. And then she'd slipped away forever. Johanna wasn't in the NICU. At over seven pounds, she was a full-term, beautiful little girl with clenched fists and a button nose, but seeing her brought so much flooding back. And then, walking in, spotting his son curled in Lizzie's arms.

He headed to the lambing shed to relieve Wick. Corrie would call him when Zeke woke up. After a snack, she'd noted, as she packed fresh cookies into a zipped bag for him.

"Hey, boss." Wick had been bent over a

stall wall, monitoring a fresh delivery. He straightened, rubbed the small of his back, but kept smiling. "Harve and Rosie are doing all right, I hear?"

"You hear right. Mother, baby and aging father."

Wick laughed. "Nothing like a baby to keep you young. And it's real nice to see them welcome this little girl after so long. And this little mama just presented triplets so we should red-string this one." He motioned to a ewe with a single lamb behind him. "And gift her a daughter so no one has to fight for food. If she takes it on, that is."

"I'll keep an eye on them to make sure she takes." Most sheep would accept an orphan lamb, but not all. "I'll give the baby a colostrum bottle before we shift her over." He scanned the tape markers on the stall doors, indicators of what had happened on the last shift. He whistled softly. "You've been busy."

"We're in the thick of it now, but I just fed and you should get a breather for a little while."

"I've got coffee." He set his insulated cup onto a small shelf close by. "And a fistful of cookies. I'm good."

Wick washed up in the barn sink before he went off to rest. Heath warmed a bottle slightly. He slipped into the pen, picked a female lamb and fed her the bottle. Then he marked her ear before offering her to the mother down the aisle.

The ewe had been resting comfortably, her baby at her side. She brought her head around when he deposited the little lamb alongside the day-old baby ram. Then he backed away.

The baby seemed confused. She bleated, turned and bleated again.

Her biological mother's voice answered from down the walkway. Then the new ewe leaned back and sniffed at her. She sniffed again, then looked around as if wondering how this had occurred.

Then she stood. The moment of truth had arrived. Would she clean up this newborn and feed her? Or would she chase her off to protect her original baby?

The lamb bleated again, as if pleading her case.

The older ewe nudged her with her nose. And then she began cleaning her, working the lamb's surface with her tongue, letting the newborn know it would be all right.

His mind went straight back to Lizzie, cuddling Zeke on the couch. Could a woman accept another person's child as readily? And how could a parent risk a bad pairing? Zeke was his responsibility. Would anyone else be able to love him like Heath did?

Anna would scold you and tell you to get over yourself. To get real.

The mental reminder was right. Anna had a way of setting him straight when he let worry take hold. She'd had faith in God and confidence in him when he had precious little in himself.

"Dad!" Zeke came through the lambing barn with a broad, open grin. "I had so much fun today! My Lizzie is the best babysitter in the whole world and she was so excited about my tooth!" He grinned wide to show off the gap. "It was like the best day ever!"

There was no denying the naked joy on his son's face. His grin. His excitement. "What did you guys do that tuckered you out so much?" he asked. "When I got home from the hospital, you were sacked out on the couch."

"Rosie's baby!" The little guy slapped a hand to his forehead in an almost comical move. "I almost forgot and we've been waiting so long!"

"The baby is beautiful, she's little but not as little as you were when you were born, and her name is Johanna."

"Jo-Jo." He shortened the name immediately. "Miss Lizzie made a card with me, and we're going to pick some flowers for Rosie-Posie and the baby. Just to make them smile when they come home."

"That's a great idea." And nothing he'd have thought of personally. He'd already ordered a bouquet of flowers to be delivered later in the week. He hadn't thought of personalizing it and making Zeke a part of the gift. But Lizzie had. "What else did you guys do?"

"Went on the best ride ever," Zeke told him. "I wanted to ride one of the new horses, but Miss Lizzie said no…but then she got Honey's Money all ready and we went up into the hills."

The hills?

"We went so high we could see the skinny top on the church and the old silos."

Which meant they'd gone beyond the soft green grasses and into the rockier outcropping to be able to see Shepherd's Crossing.

"And then she rode so fast across the grass that it was like flying, Dad! Like a real cowboy! And Corrie made cookies and grilled cheese and we cleaned stables and I fell asleep."

He zeroed in on one term. Flying.

Lizzie loved speed.

She was fearless around horses and just as

courageous up top, but to run a horse with Zeke on board?

Anger thrummed along his spine until his ears rang. He bit it back. It wasn't Zeke he needed to scold. It was Lizzie, and as soon as Zeke was tucked in for the night, he'd have a word with her. She could do what she liked on her own. Her skills made that a non-issue.

But when it came to Zeke, Heath's word was law and Lizzie Fitzgerald needed to understand that.

Don't dwell on the negatives in life. Focus on the positives, the good things, the blessings surrounding you. The past can be a good advisor but a bad ruler. Don't let it pull you down.

Lizzie needed the mental reminder as she worked a mare in the far field bordering the hills. She'd disappointed herself as a teen, but faith had saved her midway through college. She'd moved on from the past and worked hard to adopt Paul's message to the Philippians. *"Finally, brethren, whatsoever things are true, whatsoever things are honest, whatsoever things are just, whatsoever things are pure, whatsoever things are lovely, whatsoever things are of good report; if there be any virtue, and if there be any praise, think on these things."*

She'd adopted this verse as her family and their business crumbled around her. She worked hard to keep a positive attitude. But facing Heath dredged up her old choices. Her loss. So when he strode her way looking way grumpier than any man should that evening, she squared her shoulders. He could be grumpy all he wanted. That was his right. But no way would he be allowed to take it out on her.

"We need to talk." He stopped a few feet from her, as if preparing for battle, a battle she wasn't about to have.

"About me needing a stable hand that's accomplished at riding? Perfect. I'll start looking first thing Monday."

His brows drew down. "I got the text you sent about that, but that's not why I'm here."

"Then…why?" She kept her voice cool and her face relaxed.

"You took Zeke into the hills today."

His topic surprised her. "Yes. Of course. On Honey's Money."

"And you had her run with him on her back?"

And there it was, the sound of a hovering parent, micromanaging every tiny aspect of a kid's life. She'd seen plenty of that among her millennial friends. She hadn't expected to see it from Heath, a four-season cowboy with a strong work ethic. "Yet what other be so glorious to see? A horse, mane flying, running free." She refused to flinch beneath his dark gaze. "Your words, cowboy."

"I wrote that poem a long time ago, Liz." Hands braced on his hips, he scowled down at her and she returned the favor by staying cool and calm.

"A lifetime, Heath. That's how long ago it was."

"Listen, you did me a favor today, and I'm grateful."

"And yet, oddly, your tone of voice belies your words."

His frown deepened. "Zeke's my son. We play by my rules. If you're going to be here for a year—"

"Not *if*, Heath. I *am* here for a year, and probably longer because not only am I *good* at working horses—" she drew a little closer just to underscore her point "—I *love* working them. And I've got the business degree and acumen to make it work. And if you question my judgment about what I do with Zeke, then you need to find someone else to help watch him because no one—" she stepped forward again "—sets my rules except me. I've made it on my own for a long time and I'll continue to do so long after this initial year is up. So this is what you need to think about. If you leave that sweet boy in my care, I'll do as I think best. If that means riding into the hills and cantering through the grass, I'll do it again." She started to pivot but stopped when he said her name.

"You'd do it again?" She hadn't thought he could stand any taller, but he did. And then he folded his arms. "Over my dead body."

"Whatever it takes, Heath." She lifted her gaze and locked eyes with him in the fading light. "What form of torture is it to raise a boy on a beautiful ranch like Pine Ridge and deny him the chance to run a horse?" She met his anger with a steady voice. An even countenance. "There's almost nothing as wonderful as being up top a horse, Heath Caufield, and a cowboy like you should know that." She reached out and tapped his chest, just once. "Unless you've forgotten that, too."

And then she walked away.

Chapter Nine

The church bell began to toll a five-minute reminder the next morning, an old Shepherd's Crossing tradition. When folks lived in town, the tolling bell reminded them to step lively. Heath had just stepped out of the pickup truck when the bells began to chime.

"Yay!" Zeke threw his arms into the air. "We're here for the bells, Dad! I get so happy hearing the bells ring. And Cookie's chocolate cake makes me happy, too. But not as happy as riding with Miss Lizzie." Zeke amended his statement with a glance back, over his shoulder. "That was like the best ever."

"Ezekiel—" Talking about this now wouldn't be a good idea. He'd already decided to quietly let the subject go and make sure Justine understood the rules when she stepped in to watch Zeke the coming week.

But Zeke was on a roll and the caution in Heath's voice added no restraint. "She snuggled me so tight, and it was like having a mom, laughing and holding on to me so nothing would ever happen to me. And she said it was okay to miss my mom, because she misses her mom, too."

Holding him so tight? Missing his mom?

Heath's throat went tight. Zeke never talked about Anna. He never referred to missing his mother, but he'd shared that emotion yesterday. With Lizzie.

Zeke had started up the church steps but Heath called him back. "You had fun with Lizzie? Miss Lizzie," he corrected himself.

"It was awesome." Blue-gray eyes in a dusky face held his gaze and his heart. "When I go to school I'm going to tell all the kids about riding Honey's Money with Miss Lizzie."

Great. He'd spent five years raising the boy on his own, losing sleep and balancing things like a tightrope walker. And Lizzie breezed into town and won the kid's heart in less than two weeks.

It was like that for you, too. Back in the day. Remember? It took no time at all for you to lose your heart to her. "I expect they'll like hearing it."

"Me, too." Zeke reached for Heath's hand and held it. "But first I'll tell them that my dad is the best cowboy ever. Okay?"

Oh, man…

The boy's trust and devotion were wonderful things, but had Heath earned them? Did he deserve them?

Some days, yes. Others…not so much. And now he'd lambasted Lizzie for something he probably should have been doing with Zeke all along. Not racing the boy across fields, of course, but letting him experience the joy of being in the saddle, safe and secure, going faster than an old plodding horse would take him. "Very okay. And next time we go riding, I'll go a little faster. All right?"

"Yes!"

He owed Lizzie an apology. Another one. And it didn't take a math whiz to understand that if he needed to apologize this often, he was the common denominator in the problems.

He spotted Lizzie and Corrie sitting in the front of the sparsely populated church as he walked through the door. She wore a vest made from soft faux fur, trimmed in white, and her hair lay rich against the paler colors. Ivory sleeves covered her arms against the chilled April air, and when she stood, she brushed her hair back, behind her shoulder. Then she glanced back.

She spotted him, but didn't let her gaze linger. Not after he'd been such a moron the night before.

No, she dropped her eyes to Zeke and he hurried her way as if drawn, and Heath could do nothing but follow him to the front pew.

Zeke scrambled into place. He grinned up at her, then his father, then Lizzie again, as if being tucked between them was a treat. And when the elderly pastor began the short service, Zeke pretended to read out of Lizzie's book of prayer. And word by word, Lizzie helped him, tapping the words with one trim finger.

The aging pianist sounded the notes for a final hymn, but before the congregation could begin, the pastor raised a hand. "I need to say a few words before we go," he announced from the three steps leading to the sanctuary.

The pianist looked faintly annoyed but stopped playing. The small congregation grew quiet.

"You all know I've been having some health issues this year." He glanced around the church as people nodded.

"And that winter is tough on me like it is on some other old folks in the area. So here it is." He splayed his hands and gazed out at the thin clutch of people who'd made it a priority to come to church, and half a dozen of them were from Pine Ridge Ranch. "I'll be leaving Shepherd's Crossing in a few weeks. I'm going back to Boise, to live with my daughter. I wish I didn't have to do this," he told them. "Being here has meant a great deal to me, and I hope it's been good for all of us. But there's too much for an old man like me to do here, and that's the truth of it. I'll see you for a couple more weeks, and then…" He tried to smile but then his jaw quivered slightly and he stopped trying. "We'll say our goodbyes." He paused for several long seconds, then sighed. "The thing is…there won't be anyone coming to take my place."

Heath saw the congregation glance around nervously.

"There's not enough money to pay a proper wage, and even clergy needs to eat. I'm sorry. I truly am," he went on, then folded his hands tight across his middle. "We'll have to close the church."

"But not the bells, right, Dad?" Zeke might have thought he was whispering the words, but he wasn't. "We can still listen to the bells on Sunday, right?"

The whole church stayed silent. Waiting for

his answer? Waiting for someone to protest? To make things right?

He clutched Zeke's hand, because how could he answer such a question when he had no answers himself?

Then he stooped low. "I don't know, Zeke. I really don't know."

Zeke stared up at him, then lifted his eyes to where the bell tower stood above the front entrance. His gaze darkened and when old Ella Potts began banging on the piano with more zest than talent, Zeke didn't move, apparently wondering about the bells he loved so much. And Heath had absolutely no idea what to tell him.

The aged pastor was standing at the door when Heath came through with Zeke. Lizzie had threaded her way through the people, and when he got to the door, she'd disappeared from view. But as he approached the minister, the old man proffered a hand his way. "Can I have a minute, Heath?"

Zeke clung to Heath's right hand. He looked sad, and so did the pastor. No church. No pastor. No services. What kind of town were they left with? Was this what he wanted for his son? "I'm sorry you're not doing well, Pastor."

"Age catches up with most, one way or another," Reverend Sparks said. "I can't keep breath to preach like I should or pray like I should, and that's no good for me or the people. And with the church so small and getting smaller—" His voice faded. "And the town down on just about everything... Only a few dozen show up on Sundays now."

He was right, but the thought of no church in town didn't sit right with Heath, even if the only reason he came was the three-and-a-half foot boy by his side. "The town needs a church. Doesn't it?"

"The town needs God," replied the old man softly. "A building's just a building. A town steeped in the faith of our fathers can stand strong against adversity. But a town divided, with everyone going their own way, well, that's different, isn't it? When we serve ourselves and money, there's not a lot of room left for God."

A town divided.

Apt words for Shepherd's Crossing.

And he was as bad as any, taking care of his son, Sean's ranch, the sheep, and having little to do with the town or the people except as needed. He'd never seen that as a bad thing, but no church? No school? Not even a general store to grab a sandwich and a conversation on a rainy afternoon.

"You're a town leader now," the pastor continued. "Folks might want a meeting about what to do with the church. It's old and needs work, but the volunteer fire department is always looking for practice fires to hone their skills."

Burn the church? His gut clenched. "You can't be serious."

"This falling-down wreck isn't the church." The reverend pointed to Heath and Zeke, then to the thinning cloud of dust the other cars had left behind. "The people are the church. Without them, four square walls aren't much use. The church isn't in there, son. It's here in you. And them. In us."

The pastor leaving. Sean's death. Grazing rights revoked. Heath was surrounded by change. Too much, too fast, too soon. He wouldn't have thought of himself as an introvert, but right now he'd like to hole up at the ranch, take care of his own and let the world pass them by. But that attitude was what had gotten them into this mess in the first place. So maybe there was a message in the multiple blows.

"Do you need help getting ready, Reverend?"

"June'll see to it," he replied. "That's my daughter. She'll be here shortly after Memorial Day. I'll say my goodbyes to those that come the next few weeks. And then lock the door." He sighed, glanced at the church, then the town, and walked away on quiet feet.

A locked church.

An empty town.

A dusty street that saw little traffic.

"Surrounded by the rich, ignoring the poor." Lizzie's quiet observation interrupted his thoughts. He wasn't sure where she'd come from, but her words hit their mark. "This is a very Robin Hood–style place you've got here."

"Lizzie—"

She lifted her phone up. "My barn app's alerting me. I wanted to catch you in case your phone was turned off for service. Gotta run." She hurried to her SUV, got in and headed back toward Pine Ridge with Corrie by her side.

"Is Lizzie mad at us, Dad? At you and me?" Zeke peered up at him, eyes wide.

"No, son." He could say this honestly as he opened Zeke's door and helped the boy in. "She's not one bit mad at you. For anything."

"Well, then it might be you in big trouble," Zeke offered seriously, "'cause I think she was mad at somebody, Dad. And we're the only people here."

"We'll fix it when we get home. And I'm

going to leave you with Cookie this afternoon because Lizzie and I have to take care of a horse having a baby."

"And then I can peek at the baby when it's done?" Eagerness lifted the worry from his tone.

"You make it sound like we're cooking a turkey, not delivering a foal, but yes, you can come look. As long as you're quiet."

"I will be!"

Jace was exiting the first barn as Zeke scrambled out of the rear seat. He moved Heath's way and paused. "Two things, and you're not going to like either one of them so let me apologize first."

Jace's troubled look underscored the words.

"Justine isn't available to watch the little guy like we planned. She got an offer of a paid internship in Seattle and can't turn it down so she's staying in Seattle for at least six weeks. She tried calling you but your cell went straight to voice mail and your mailbox is full. She feels terrible because she knows this leaves you in a lurch, but the offer just came through."

He'd turned his phone off before church, and hadn't noticed the missed call when he turned it back on. "She's sure, Jace? Because this puts us in a spot we can't afford to be in."

He'd managed to insult Lizzie's child care abilities, Cookie wouldn't take kindly to nonstop child duty and Corrie hadn't come north to play nanny. Although she'd be a great one.

"I know. But wait, Heath. It gets worse."

He watched his friend struggle for words, and Heath was pretty sure he didn't want to hear whatever Jace was going to say next.

"I'm leaving."

Heath swallowed hard. Jace was great on the ranch, but ranching wasn't his primary job. He was a skilled carpenter: he'd overseen the building of the last two barns and he'd honed his reputation on Pine Ridge properties, but with the area's diminishing population, there weren't enough jobs to keep him busy. And he was Heath's closest friend.

"I love working here and living here," Jace went on. His gaze wandered the ranch, then lingered on the hills beyond. "My family helped build this town over a hundred years ago, and there weren't too many black ranchers in these parts. Or anywhere. But things have gone downhill and I've got to go where there's work. I'm going to sell my parents' place and use that money to pay off Justine's schooling and stake my business."

His parents had passed away just over a

year apart when Justine started college three years before. "You going to Sun Valley?"

"Where else?"

The rising fortunes of the picturesque central valley had drawn a lofty tourism trade while home values pitched up. Folks in Sun Valley would have the means to hire a guy like Jace and pay him what he was worth.

"I've looked the situation over every which way, but it seems like the only option on the table right about now. It'll take some time to sell our place," he added. "There aren't folks lined up to buy houses around here, so plan on me being here at least a month. Maybe more. I'm sorry, Heath." Jace tipped his cowboy hat back slightly. "This wasn't how I saw things going. We've been friends for a dozen years, and I never thought it would go down like this but my hands are tied."

They'd had plans as younger men. Thoughts about how to resuscitate the town, how to bring back jobs and hope. But the plans went on hold as the ranch grew. Sean's vision and dreams kept them both busy, and they'd forged ahead without seeing the whole picture. Now it was too late.

"I get it, Jace. You know I do. A man's got to have work and you're too good a builder to spend your life running sheep."

"I like working the ranch well enough. I'd like to have my own spread someday, a Middleton ranch like my great-grandpa had. That was always my dream." Jace shrugged. "But I'm meant to hold a hammer and run a saw, and I knew that from the time my daddy taught me everything he'd learned. It's not even just wanting to do it. It's *needing* to do it. I just never thought I'd be doing it away from here."

Heath understood completely. It wasn't about the money or the power of heading up a high-priced property. It was about taking the right trail to get where you were going.

Lizzie texted just then. Maybe labor, maybe not. Nothing much happening. Will keep you posted.

OK, he texted back,

"I'll turn the established pairs onto the meadow." Once a ewe established her little family with strong nursing instincts, they were turned onto a select nearby pasture to eat, grow and socialize, making room for more newborn lambs. Head down, Jace moved toward the lambing shed.

Heath turned toward the stables. Lizzie didn't need him if the horse wasn't laboring, and he had plenty to do, but he owed her an apology for his outburst the day before.

She'd put a light in his son's eyes, and he'd squelched things by hitting the panic button. Now he had to eat his words because Rosie wouldn't be able to watch Zeke for weeks.

He texted Cookie to keep an eye on Zeke for the time being. That meant the little guy had to stay inside on a brilliant spring day because Cookie had jobs to do.

Guilt rose within him but that had become more normal than not. Did all single parents face these dilemmas? He wouldn't know because he'd become very good at insulating himself. Just like Sean.

He walked into the barn, crossed to the office wing and tapped on Lizzie's door. She turned, surprised, then pointed up toward the monitor on the wall. "Nothing much happening. Didn't you get my text?"

"I did." He walked into the room, shoved his hands into his pockets, then pulled them right back out again. "I didn't come because of the mare. I came to apologize."

Apologize? She stood, faced him, then folded her arms. "I'm listening."

Gorgeous eyes gazed into hers, as if searching.

"I was out of line yesterday and I'm sorry."

She lifted a brow slightly but stayed quiet

because he was right. He was out of line and no one got to treat her that way. Ever.

"I should have been glad you took Zeke for a ride. I know your skills, I know your instincts, I know you. I let old buttons get pushed and that was plain stupid."

Still she waited, unwilling to offer him help or absolution.

"It's been crazy busy here, not just since Sean died but since he got sick. I haven't had time to do things I should with Zeke, and Rosie had her hands full. She was pregnant and watching Zeke and a set of twins."

"Zeke told me about the twins. I think he felt trapped because Rosie was busy and he couldn't do too much outside."

"Rosie said as much. I just figured it would all work out in time, but it didn't. It was winter and then Sean started to go downhill. That increased the workload on me, but I did it at the expense of my son. Now I'm not sure how to undo any of it."

"Delegate?"

He brought his chin up quickly.

"You trust the people working with you to handle vital things, but when it comes to Zeke, fear gets in the way. Trust more and worry less," she told him.

"Easier said than done."

She laughed. He scowled, and that only made her laugh more. "You know those birds of the air? The fish in the sea? Those sparrows that God cares for every single day? Be more like them," she suggested. "Trust. Reach out. There is life beyond Pine Ridge Ranch, just like there was life beyond Fitzgerald News. It's a question of exploring it. Then embracing it."

She glanced up at the monitor, saw nothing of note, and eased a hip onto the office desk. "Zeke loves being on the ranch. He's a born cowboy. But he could use some time with his daddy to figure out how to be the best cowboy he can be. And if you can't take him with you off the ranch because time is short right now, make him your sidekick. When it's safe. It will do you both good. And while I appreciate the apology..." She moved a step closer, determined to make her point. "Nobody gets to go off on me like that, Heath. Ever. Don't do it again."

If her reprimand surprised him, he didn't show it. "I won't. Most of the time." He sent her a rueful grin, a look she remembered like it was yesterday, the kind of grin that stole a young girl's heart. "I get stupid about Zeke sometimes."

"Loving your child isn't stupid. It's how it's

supposed to be. Every kid in the world should have at least one parent who loves them."

Sympathy softened his jaw. His gaze. "Your father's a moron, Lizzie. And selfish. I'm sorry he messed you girls up."

"We're educated. We're smart. We'll be okay. But he cost over a thousand people their jobs and their pensions while he lives the life of a rich man in Dubai on stolen capital. That's indefensible. And he got away with it." She frowned. "I honestly don't know how he lives with himself."

"And that's why Sean named you three women in the will. He couldn't believe what his brother did to you. How he left the three of you holding the bag and some pretty stiff college loans for Charlotte and Mel."

She was tired of rehashing her father's misdeeds. "Just be glad you ended up working for this Fitzgerald brother. That he gave you a chance. Because I can see you love this place, Heath."

"It saved me." He turned his gaze outward. "I owe Sean and I owe this ranch, and no one expected him to get sick. To die. So the fact that he left me part of all this humbles me. And challenges me. So yeah." He stood, tall and strong, shoulders back. "I love it. And I have to do whatever it takes to continue its success."

"That's when I call on my faith," she told him quietly. "To give me the strength I need."

He looked at her. Right at her. And he didn't blink an eye. "The work of human hands has gotten me a whole lot farther than some intangible belief system. Diving in, getting things done, staying the course."

"Except that you were just in church with me a couple of hours ago. Somehow this doesn't compute."

"I always take Zeke to church. His mother isn't here to do it, so I do it in her place. She'd have wanted me to. It was important to her."

But not to him.

The ring he still wore on his left hand gleamed brighter when a stray sunbeam hit the corner of the office window. It made a perfect reminder for Lizzie.

Heath didn't do change well. He depended on himself and few others, and most assuredly not God.

She depended on God for everything. He'd been with her throughout the dark days after her father discovered her pregnancy. The shunning she'd received from her illustrious grandfather. And He'd been with her when she'd called on Heath for help, and Heath had ignored her pleas.

She folded her hands lightly in her lap. "I don't know where I'd be today without my faith, Heath. It's been my mainstay when people let me down. When man failed me, God stood watch. I'm sorry it hasn't been that way for you because I remember when you used to go to church every Sunday and pray for your father."

"A fat lot of good that did me."

She heard the pain in his voice. She understood how hard it was to grow up happy when parents fail in their job of simply loving their children. She'd had money and stature to fall back on.

Heath had a drunken father in a dirty stable apartment.

She wouldn't argue with him. Or try and convince him. He needed to find his own path back to faith, on his own terms. But she could pray for him to find the peace and joy God wanted for him. The quiet contentment she wanted for him.

His phone buzzed a text. He read it and moved to the door. "Jace needs a hand."

Would he go get Zeke and let the little fellow pal around in the sheep barn? Or was he expecting others to take charge and keep Zeke under lock and key for the duration?

"I'll keep you apprised of what's going on here."

"I'd appreciate it." And before she could make a face behind his back, he turned. "Not because I don't trust you to do it, Liz. But so I don't thoroughly mess up if I have to step up to the plate someday."

"A good plan. See you later."

He cut across the grass to the house to throw some work clothes on.

She stared up at the cloudless sky, wondering how anyone could live here and not see the beauty of God's creation. Or believe in God Himself.

Could she help Heath? Or would drawing close to him again simply draw her into his work-first world?

She didn't know, but when he came out of the house and headed to the sheep barn without Zeke, she was disappointed.

Sure, there was risk on a ranch. There was risk everywhere. But if Heath used all his time working solo instead of bringing his little boy with him whenever possible, he wasn't just building a ranch. He was building a wall between father and son, a wall that didn't need to exist except when fear grabbed hold and wouldn't let go.

And that might be the worst wall of all.

Chapter Ten

Heath returned to the stables when she texted him in the late afternoon. "I got your message. How's she doing?"

"We've got hooves showing."

"That's quick. And she's handling it well?"

"This isn't her first rodeo," replied Lizzie as she jotted notes into the electronic notebook. She'd set up a small table around the corner from the foaling mare. It held a tall iced tea in a plastic bottle and a container of Corrie's homemade cookies, the closest she'd come to food all day. "She's had two other successful foals. And one stillbirth."

Heath had been watching the monitor above him. He stopped watching and turned her way. "Sean bought a horse with a thirty-three percent failure rating?"

Lizzie's heart went tight. So did her hands.

And when she found the breath to address his statement she kept her voice soft on purpose. "I don't think the horse considered it a failure. I think she saw it as a loss, Heath."

Her reply flustered him. Good.

"I don't mean she failed, that was a stupid way to put it. We have lamb losses. Their percentages get higher if the weather turns, or if we get an attack of scours. There are so many factors that affect newborns that we're constantly watching during lambing season. But with a horse it's one foal every two years and when you lose one out of three, that's a higher percentage than Sean would have normally entertained."

He made sense but that didn't erase the sting of the word "failure." "Let's just say they might not have been forthcoming about the stillbirth. I found it accidentally when I was examining records. Maybe Uncle Sean only saw what they wanted him to see. Or maybe he wanted her to have another chance. A happier one."

He seemed to miss the latter part of her statement and bore directly into the first half. "They falsified records?"

"It wasn't in the paperwork so unless they told him verbally, then yes. By omission," she added. "But right now let's focus on them."

A nose appeared between the two thick hooves, and within twenty minutes they had a blue roan colt on the ground, one of the most majestic colts she'd ever seen.

"Oh, he's a stunner." Lizzie breathed the words, watching. "A classic beauty. And with a lineage that puts him into a class all his own. So maybe Uncle Sean did know about the lost foal." She leaned on the adjoining stall gate, watching the pair bond. "But he saw Josie's potential and bought her anyway."

"That's a big chance to take on a whole lot of investment," said Heath, but then his next words eased the sting. "And well worth every penny. Like I said before, you and Sean have an eye for horses. And an ear. I'm making a pledge right now that I won't interfere with your decisions. Mostly."

"And I'll promise to ignore you as needed. Mostly."

She tipped a smile up his way, then paused.

Their eyes met. Held. Lingered.

His gaze dropped to her mouth. Stayed there. And then he reached out one finger to her cheek. Just one. He traced the curve of her cheek with that one finger as if remembering. Or maybe reminding himself of what they'd had way back when.

The sound of the stable door clicking shut

pulled them apart, and when Corrie turned down the alley with Zeke, Lizzie was studiously watching mother and baby, which was what she should have been doing all along.

She turned to welcome Heath's son and focused on the boy's excitement. "Hey, little man. The baby is here and he's beautiful."

"I'm so happy he's here!" Zeke kept his voice quiet. He peeked into the stall when Heath lifted him into his arms. "Isn't he like the coolest baby horse ever?"

"He is a rare beauty," noted Corrie, but she sent Lizzie a sharp look. A look that Lizzie refused to acknowledge. "He might be your second-generation stallion if you keep him. That color alone is worth a fair price."

"We'll see how he musters up, but yes." Lizzie hung back with them so they wouldn't spook the mother. "He's a looker."

"He sure is. I'm going up to take care of some overdue office work up front," Heath said. He faced Corrie. "Are you okay with Zeke for a while?"

Corrie shook her head. "Unfortunately, no. We've had a nice afternoon, but Cookie and I are laying plans for the vegetable garden. But I'll see you both at supper."

He started to turn toward Lizzie. The mare whinnied, a reminder that Lizzie was on the job, too. "Well, bud, you'll have to tag along with me."

Zeke pressed a kiss to his father's cheek. "I love that, Dad!"

Heath's expression relaxed. "Me, too. We'll see you ladies later."

"Wonderful." Corrie smiled, but when he was out of sight, she turned to Lizzie with a more thoughtful expression. "You guard your head. He guards his heart." She drawled the words intentionally. "How can this possibly work, darlin'?"

"There's nothing to work," Lizzie told her.

Corrie sniffed. "You couldn't fool me then, you can't fool me now. And it's not that I don't understand the attraction. Heath Caufield is a fine man. And he carries himself tall and strong, but there's a world of hurtin' in those big blue eyes and you've had enough of that, I think."

"Corrie…"

Corrie raised both hands up, palms out. "I'm not interfering."

"Mmm-hmm." Lizzie drew the wheelbarrow closer for stall cleaning.

"But I'm not afraid to protect my own, Lizzie-Beth. I might have failed in that before. I don't aim to fail now."

Concern drew Corrie's brows together and

Lizzie knew the sincerity of the sweet nanny's words. But she wasn't a wayward teen any longer. "I'm all grown up, Corrie. And pretty independent."

"Tell this old woman something I don't know."

Lizzie grinned and looped an arm around Corrie's shoulders in a half hug. "You're not old. You're seasoned. And I'd be lying to say there isn't an attraction. The kid is a total bonus. But I will never settle for less than the whole thing again, Corrie. Faith, hope and love. Heath's so mad at God and life that whatever faith he had is gone and he wears his wedding ring like a badge of honor. I decided a long time ago that I'll never take second place again. And I meant it."

"So we wait and see while we work here. Maybe the good Lord has brought us to Idaho to make a difference. Your uncle's generosity has opened a door for us. Perhaps there's a way to open a door for others."

Lizzie envisioned the worn-out town, the thinning population and the problems surrounding them. "I don't know how, Corrie."

"Then we pray for vision." Corrie squeezed her hand lightly. "The little man and I made spoon bread to go with supper. If we bring some Southern cooking and hospitality into the deep north, it's bound to have some kind of effect. It can't hurt anything more than it's already hurting."

Southern cooking.

Hospitality.

Lizzie worked those thoughts around in her head once Corrie went back to the house.

How could people work together if they never came together? And what brought most people out?

Weddings and funerals.

Since there wasn't a wedding in the plans, she sought Heath out that evening, once Zeke was in bed. "Got a minute?"

"Before I fall asleep?" He'd been checking something on his phone. He put it away. "Yes."

"You said Uncle Sean was cremated."

"He wanted his ashes returned to the ranch he loved. Yes."

"Is there a memorial?"

He frowned. "A what?"

"A grave. A marker. Something to commemorate his life."

"I think the ranch is a pretty big marker. Don't you?"

"No." The night had taken a strong dip in temperature so she pulled her hoodie closer. "Uncle Sean was a decorated marine. He was awarded the Navy Cross and a Purple Heart. He saved three men from an ambush and took a bullet to the leg while dragging them, one at a time, to safety. The farm is a great legacy. But a memorial is a better reminder of that sacrifice."

He took her words seriously. "I've never thought of that. You mean like put a place in the cemetery? For us to buy a plot?"

She shook her head. "Why not right here on the land he loved?"

"Listen, this is a great idea, it really is, but I don't have time to organize something like this during lambing. I wouldn't even know how to."

"I'll do it."

He still looked hesitant, but Lizzie pressed her point. "It's the right thing to do, Heath."

"It is. I'm just embarrassed we didn't think of it ourselves."

"And now we did. Zeke and I will get on it first thing tomorrow."

"About Zeke—"

"Yes?"

He worked his jaw slightly. "Do you mind helping with him the next few weeks?"

She should refuse. Heath was way too protective and she found that stifling and fairly annoying. But he was caught in a jam. He'd done the responsible thing and had arranged child care, then got thwarted at the last minute. She couldn't fault him for that. "I'll help as I'm able. Between you and me and Corrie, we should be able to keep one five-year-old out of mischief for a while."

He covered her hands with one of his, the one sporting a plain gold band. "Thanks, Liz."

She kept her smile light and her tone easy. "That's what friends are for." She withdrew her hands from his and headed for the stables, but first she checked the dog food dish out back.

More food was gone, but there was no sign of the bedraggled dog. She whistled lightly, hoping it would come but nothing moved in the growing darkness.

At least the little dog was getting regular meals. She understood Heath's concern about animals and disease control, but kindness mattered, too.

So the food dish stayed right where it was.

Chapter Eleven

Two hundred and forty-three lambs and they weren't half done, but their results were promising, and that was a weight off Heath's shoulders.

His phone rang midmorning. He glanced down, chose to ignore the call and shoved the phone back into his pocket.

"Melos again?" asked Jace.

Heath grunted. A sheep farmer from farther down the valley wanted to raise a ruckus over the change in grazing rights.

Heath didn't have time for a ruckus, and he'd said that outright, but Blake Melos was persistent. "They're having a meeting tomorrow night. Who's got time to have meetings this time of year?" he asked.

Jace kept cleaning lambing stalls to prepare for the next wave. "If you want to have a neighbor, you've got to be a neighbor."

Heath growled but Jace was good at ignoring his growls. Today was no exception. "Like it or not, you don't exist in a vacuum here. Pine Ridge Ranch isn't an entity unto itself. It's part of something bigger. A town. A community. And if no one starts caring about that, then what do we have left?" The sound of the pitchfork hitting concrete punctuated his point. "Every fix begins somewhere. Getting together with these people is a smart thing to do. Sean lived on his own for a lot of reasons," Jace reminded him. "But he probably should have reached out more. And Carrington, with his monster-sized spread, flying in and out on his private landing strip." Jace waved toward south where Eric Carrington was developing a celebrated Angus cattle operation with his family's pharmaceutical fortune. "If the big players on the board ignore the good of the community, pretty soon there is no community."

Which was what they were facing now.

Jace was right. He didn't have to like being involved in this group of angry ranchers, but it was the right thing to do. He texted Blake a quick message. I'll be there.

Then he pushed the phone back into his pocket.

"I'll go with you," said Jace. "Wick will be on barn duty then. And Lizzie should go, too."

"It's got nothing to do with horses."

"And everything to do with joining forces. Like it or not, she's part of the force."

That was another problem, because he did like it. He liked it a lot. She didn't let him get so caught up in himself or the ranch that he couldn't see beyond it, and that hadn't happened in—

So long that he couldn't remember. He'd been putting his shoulder to the wheel since setting foot on Pine Ridge soil, but maybe it wasn't a question of working harder. Maybe it came down to working smarter.

Corrie had been with Zeke that morning. Lizzie was taking the afternoon as long as the remaining mares stayed quiet. He walked up to the house midafternoon. Zeke should be napping and he'd have a few minutes of quiet time with Lizzie.

That thought made him walk a little quicker, but when he kicked off his barn boots and came through to the kitchen, Zeke wasn't napping. He was perched on one of the tall stools, making a cake. With Lizzie. And the sight of them, laughing together, daubing frosting onto the cake, softened another corner of his heart.

"Did I miss someone's birthday?" he asked.

Zeke slipped off the tall stool as if he were a much bigger kid and dashed toward his father. "Nope. Lizzie and me—"

"Lizzie and I." The two adults corrected him in unison, and then they smiled. At the same time. At one another, with the miniature cowboy grinning between them, almost as if it was supposed to be that way.

"Lizzie and I," Zeke corrected himself, sounding bored with the effort. He beamed at his father. Frosting smeared his shirt and the back of his hands. "My Lizzie said we're making a cake just acause."

"*Because*," she told him. "Because we can and we thought everyone would really, really love cake."

"Because it's so delicious! Right, Dad?"

Heath reached out and swiped a finger along the edge of the frosting bowl and tasted it. "It is amazingly delicious."

"And now Zeke is going to decorate the cake," said Lizzie. She held up a plastic cone half-filled with frosting. "Remember how we practiced? Hold the bag tight with one hand and squeeze with the other."

"I will." He scrambled back to his seat, grinning.

"Don't lick your fingers like I did," warned Heath. "You're fixing this for other folks to eat, so you've got to be careful."

Lizzie didn't mention that Zeke may have already licked his fingers a time or two. "Blake Melos called the house phone twice. He left two messages. Which means he's probably calling your cell and you're ignoring him."

"Was ignoring him," he corrected her. "I texted him that I'd be at the meeting, although the diminished grazing bill is a done deal. I don't see the good in talking it to death. Not when we're so bogged down in work right here."

She handed Zeke a bottle of spring-colored sprinkles that Heath was pretty sure were a new addition to the kitchen, because Cookie wasn't a sprinkle kind of guy.

"I've been here a long time now," he went on, "and most folks here mind their own business."

"Which could explain the failing town," she noted as she watched Zeke's attempts to squiggle frosting onto the cake. "I've never lived in a small town, but I'm pretty sure folks are supposed to rally together when things are rough. Aren't they?"

"You've got big game hunting and tourism on one side of this issue and failing sheep farms on the other. Beef is taking over and that lessens the effect of anything the sheep ranchers might say and hay's battling it out with potatoes as the top crop. Why get into a war we can't win?"

"Because maybe the other ranches don't have the means to switch things up and need that hill grazing to survive. This place is well-established and had money for a solid start. Not everyone has that option." She was guiding Zeke's hand to keep at least some of the frosting on the cake, but shifted those pretty eyes up to him. "If no one's producing market lambs for the West Coast, you've got a lot of disappointed customers. A lot of ethnic celebrations use lamb as part of their festivities. Pointing out the beneficial factors to the governor might not be a bad idea. I'd be glad to write the letter for you."

He tensed instantly. "I can write my own letter."

"So why use the journalist to help?" She made a face of pretend surprise. "My bad."

"My Lizzie helped me write a letter, Dad."

Zeke kept on dotting the white-frosted cake with yellow blobs. "She's a good teacher."

His Lizzie? Heath drew his brows down, good and tight. "You mean Miss Lizzie."

"Well, I keep forgetting that part, and I like saying my Lizzie." Zeke flashed a smile at Lizzie and leaned his dark head against Liz's side. "She teaches me lots of things. Like how to write letters. So maybe you should let her help you, too." He beamed a smile up at Liz, then pointed to the far end of the table. "That's my first letter, Dad! And it's for you!"

Heath crossed to the table and picked up the sheet of paper. He read it, then turned back to her. To Zeke. "You helped him write this?"

"I helped him with spelling." Lizzie bumped shoulders with the boy. "I was working on my things while he was working on his. Didn't he do a marvelous job?"

"It's beautiful." Heath stared at the paper, then his son. He didn't want to get emotional over something so simple, but he did because his kid had just written him a letter. "I don't know what to say, Zeke. Thank you."

"It says *I Love You Dad*," Zeke declared from his spot on the stool. "And I do! I love you this much!" He spread his arms, but forgot to set the bag down. Sun-toned frosting dribbled onto the floor.

"Oops." Lizzie grabbed a couple of paper towels while Heath picked up a washcloth. They both bent to clean up the mess, a swirl of neon gold soaking into their respective wipes.

And then their hands touched.

Paused.

"Liz." Heath didn't just say her name. He whispered it in a voice that begged a question, a question with no answers. He covered her hand with his, and whispered her name again.

She raised her eyes.

The look of him. His scent, the messed up hair, the ruggedness of a man unafraid to work the land long hours, day into night…

Did she lean closer?

Did he?

She didn't know, but the temptation drew her in.

She pulled back quickly.

What was she thinking? Doing? She knew better.

"Our young helper made a little mess?" Corrie's cheerful voice severed the moment. "Heath, you'll need hot water and drops of dish soap to get the grease off the floor. We don't want anyone slipping, and I've just been over to see Rosie and that new baby." Corrie laid a hand to her chest as if to swoon, Southern woman to the max. "My heart, my heart, to hold one that small, and so perfect. I told them about the ceremony we'd like to do for Sean's marker at the end of the month. Land sakes, she was excited. They'd like to wait for the men to come out of the hills, but that's a long way off. When I mentioned Memorial Day, both she and Harve thought that was a good idea."

"Good." Lizzie didn't look at Corrie. She didn't look at Heath, either. She didn't dare, because what would she see?

She didn't know, and wasn't sure she wanted to know.

He'd stood up when Corrie walked in. He crossed to the sink, rinsed out the cloth, then heated it with hotter water and a little soap. He cleaned up the spill thoroughly, then tossed the cloth into a laundry room hamper before he grabbed a sandwich from the tray in the fridge.

Nothing in his manner suggested they'd shared anything other than a wipe-the-spot moment.

"You're okay with the pest for a while more?"

His teasing made Zeke grin.

"We've got some errands to run, so yes. We're double-teaming the memorial project."

"After his nap?" Heath asked.

"My Lizzie says I'm getting too big for naps." Zeke drew his brow into a frown so much like Heath's, it made Lizzie smile.

"Corrie's advice," said Lizzie. "And I never argue with Corrie." She shared a smile with the older woman. "Not when it comes to raising wonderful kids. And I believe my exact words were that you won't be needing a nap every day," she corrected him. "Because you'll be off to school soon and there are no naps in school."

"That's four months away. And little kids need their sleep."

"'Zactly, Dad." Zeke offered his father a sage look. "But big kids don't hardly need them at all. And 'member how you said I'm a big kid now? When I turned five?"

Heath looked trapped by his own words, and Lizzie kind of liked that. "I think the grown-ups around you will take it day by day. Flexibility is good. And right now we need to finish this cake, my friend, and get out of Cookie's way. He's due back from the market any minute."

"Okay!"

* * *

She'd made a pretty picture standing there, a smudge of white frosting on her right cheek. She'd tucked her hair up in some kind of clip, and the pale, freckled skin of her arm, curved around Zeke but not touching him, showed a protective instinct that surprised him but shouldn't because he'd known her gentle heart for years.

He set a ladder up along the back of the barn farthest from the house. Winter winds had loosened shingles on a lean-to addition, and heavy rain and winds were predicted. Damp conditions played havoc with newborn lambs. He pulled old shingles and tossed them into the bed of a pickup below, but no matter how hard he worked, he couldn't unravel the mix of threads running through his head.

Landowners had largely ignored the town, and as online services and shopping improved, they'd gone into Shepherd's Crossing for little more than church and to pay the taxes. Then the local government had made it possible to pay taxes online, so for the past couple of years now a click of a button took care of that.

He wanted to help.

Not just help.

He wanted to fix things, to make it better.

And to do that, he needed help. Or maybe just needed to be a help. Tomorrow's meeting might be a good place to start.

It felt odd to include others on Pine Ridge business, but it no longer felt wrong, and that was a step forward.

An out-of-place sound grabbed his attention. A dog, he thought, where no dog should be. He stood up, peering left, then right.

The sound came again, fainter this time, moving away from the sheep and the lambs.

He saw nothing, but stray dogs were a rarity here. They posed a danger to sheep. A malicious dog could wreak havoc with a flock. The Maremma sheepdog hadn't barked, and all seemed well in the nursing pasture. They'd moved the sheep and lambs up one field that morning to avoid soggy ground following the rain, and all seemed calm.

His thumb went to the ring finger on his left hand, the reminder of what he'd had and lost. As it did, Lizzie's SUV pulled away from the house, with Zeke in the back seat.

He wasn't sure if his heart ached or stretched just then, but it did something it hadn't done in a long while. It opened. It opened to the thought of opportunities he'd never expected and didn't know he'd want until Lizzie had stepped foot on the ranch.

He slipped the ring into his pocket, then pushed the odd feeling away. His hand would grow accustomed to not having a ring in time. And he needed to be open to the changes around him. *All* the changes, he reminded himself.

"Need help up there?" Jace asked from below.

"I wouldn't say no."

Jace climbed the ladder quickly. "Wick's in the barn, Harve texted me that he's going stir-crazy already, and we can get this done this afternoon if we double-team it."

He literally didn't know what he'd do without Jace when the man left, because there was nothing Jace couldn't put his hand to on the ranch. "Let's do it."

By the time they finished stripping the shingles, the wind had shifted. A rim of dark clouds edged the western horizon, meaning they better move quickly.

"You cut, I'll shingle," said Jace, and Heath didn't argue. They worked in tandem, heads down, as the storm front approached, so when the sound of a tractor came out of nowhere two hours later, Heath stood.

Lizzie and Zeke were rumbling up the farm lane leading south. He was on her lap, holding the steering wheel of the small, older tractor, and she was guiding the rig with her hands over his.

Zeke looked up, saw Heath and tried to stand while the tractor kept moving forward. "Dad! Look at me! I'm driving a tractor!"

He didn't think. He didn't pause. He climbed down the ladder. He hit the ground running, and when he raced around the edge of the barn, he doubled his pace to get in front of the tractor up the gentle grade. He squared himself in the path, held up one hand and said "Stop."

Lizzie stopped.

She stared at him and rolled her eyes, but she stopped. Of course the other option would be to run him over, and the flash in her eyes indicated it might have crossed her mind.

"Come here." He moved to the tractor's side and reached for Zeke.

"But I'm riding with my Lizzie." Zeke looked surprised and pretty indignant. "We are going to see what's at the top of the hill and then make pictures of what we see from up there."

"You could have taken a four-by-four with seatbelts," Heath scolded her. "You could have walked. You could have made a choice that put my son's safety first, Liz. But you didn't."

She locked eyes with him.

He'd infuriated her. He saw that.

But then he saw something else, something worse.

Pity.

He didn't think he could get angrier, but he did.

He didn't need her pity or her sympathy. He was fine. Just fine. She was the one out of line.

He hauled Zeke into his arms and strode back to the house. Zeke cried all the way. He cried for Lizzie. He cried for his tractor ride, sounding like the tired boy he had to be.

He took him into the house, tucked him into bed, then ignored Zeke's anger until the boy fell into a troubled sleep.

Corrie said nothing to him. Not one word. But her silence spoke volumes.

Cookie arched a brow, but he stayed quiet, too.

Why was Heath the bad guy in all this? Why did everyone think they would be better at raising his child than he was?

He stomped back to the roof once Zeke fell asleep.

"Oh, you are in it now, my friend." Jace muttered the words as Heath began handing him full-sized shingles. "I expect folks all the way in town heard that child carrying on, and the poor sheep were racing this way and that, wondering what the ruckus was about."

"They were not." He knew how important it was to keep sheep calm. They were placid creatures, but once riled, they tended to stay upset.

"Perhaps racing is too strong a term, but you got their attention. You know that was one of the things I loved about my daddy," Jace continued. He waved the hammer toward the farm lane. "He'd set me right up on that tractor seat and talk to me while he worked. He showed me every little thing there was to know about working a farm, riding herd, running equipment. I don't remember an age where I wasn't part of his work detail, so when he died in that mudslide, it was like a part of me died, too. But I don't have a view in these parts that doesn't remind me of him. In the hills, on a roof, in a pew each and every Sunday or framing walls. Jason Middleton might not have lived as long as we would have liked, but he lived every minute he had, teaching me and Justine how to do things. And when he wasn't able to be there, my mama wasn't afraid to take the reins and do the same thing."

A part of Heath wanted Jace to shut up. Another part knew he was right.

"You got mad at God a long time ago," Jace noted. He didn't stop hammering, and the pneumatic gun shot nails with a steady ping! ping! ping! as Heath laid shingles. "Anna knew it. Yeah, she talked to me about it," he said when Heath gave him a sharp look. "She prayed for you. I expect Lizzie'll pray for you, too. In time." He bent low again, nailing shingles with quick precision. "If she doesn't kill you first."

They finished the roof in silence.

Lizzie had told him to delegate. He hadn't listened, not really. And it wasn't just where Zeke was concerned, although that was a major issue.

He was turning into a micromanager, not trusting folks to do their jobs and that was no way to run a busy ranch. Overseeing was one thing.

Being a bossy jerk was quite another.

I will not kill him.
I will not kill him.
I will not—

Lizzie ran the pledge through her head while she drove the tractor back to the equipment shed.

The little guy had been perfectly safe in her arms on the wide-seated tractor. She'd learned to run tractor in Kentucky, not because she needed to learn that stuff. That was what farm staff was for on a sprawl like Claremorris.

She'd learned it because she loved working the land and working with horses, because showing, riding and caring for horses was part of her Celtic blood, and because she was born to it, just like she was born to run a business. God had gifted her with both talents.

Did Heath know this? Or was he assuming a greenhorn was taking his kid on a death-defying adventure?

The hammering on the roof stopped as she parked the tractor. She crossed to the stables. She wasn't ready to have a face-off with Heath. In the peace of the horse barn she could work, think and pray.

And then she'd kill him.

That thought cheered her as she rounded the stable, but she hadn't paused to peek around the corner and her quick approach startled the scruffy dog.

It jumped up, barked twice and raced off toward the walk-in shed at the back of the first horse pasture. It darted out of sight like it had done before and she rued the lost opportunity to coax the dog closer.

"Was that a stray dog?"

She hadn't heard Heath approach, and she wasn't all that pleased with him so his tough tone of voice didn't sit well. "Not a stray anymore."

He glanced to the food and water dish, then surprised her because he didn't scold. He sighed. "It's different here, Liz."

Right, cowboy. Tell me something I don't know.

"Sheep view dogs as wolves. The Border collies and the Maremmas are raised with them. That's why we keep them in the field, not in the house. They're here to do a very important job as guardians. But stray dogs can make sheep crazy, and crazy sheep lose lambs. They stop feeding, they get nervous, and that nervousness spreads through a flock. It's not that I'm against being nice to animals. It's that the wrong dog can mess up a flock real quick. We'll have to catch that one." He thrust his chin toward the shed. "And there's a lot to lose if he starts bothering the horses. Had you considered that?"

Of course she had, hence the coaxing. But he wasn't scolding. He was...talking. And that eased the edge off her earlier ire. "Catch him and do what with him?"

Heath frowned. "We could start with a bath."

She almost smiled. "I noticed that, too."

"And then take it from there. How long have you been feeding him?"

"A while," she admitted.

"Ah." He smiled then, a true smile, the kind she knew and loved back in Kentucky. "Listen, Liz…"

She waited.

He rocked back on his heels and rubbed his jaw like he always did when he thought too hard. "I shouldn't have interfered with you and Zeke. I just—"

"Get scared to death over things you can't control and lash out irrationally?"

"I was going to say I overreact when I get worried, but your take works, too."

She thrust her hands into her pockets as the cold front rolled in. "You are embarrassing yourself and me when you act like that. It's got to stop."

He didn't deny it. But he didn't look happy, either.

"Is this how you treat Rosie when she cares for Zeke? As if she's incapable of handling a busy five-year-old?"

"I would if she pulled dangerous stunts with my son involved. She doesn't. Nor would she."

Lizzie raised a hand to thwart him. "First of all, learning to ride with an expert rider isn't exactly letting the boy set off fireworks or juggle steak knives. And seeing the workings of machinery first-hand, for a little guy who loves Mega Machines and constantly asks to watch it on his tablet, is a no-brainer. If you were giving him a tractor ride, I suppose it would be all right?"

"I'm his father."

"Except you're busy, you've taken on a huge responsibility here, you're short on help and you've got more irons in the fire than a beef ranch branding party. Let's cut to the chase. You don't trust me. But it's not just me, Heath," she added, facing him. "It's everyone, except my uncle, maybe. And he's gone."

He flinched.

"You didn't used to be this untrusting and get angry over things. I don't know this Heath Caufield." She pointed to him. "But I know one thing. The other Heath Caufield was one of the best men I ever had the privilege to know. I'd like to see that one more often."

He stared beyond her to the deepening twilight, made denser by the dense clouds. "I didn't know you could drive a tractor."

She arched one brow, waiting.

"I saw you driving, then Zeke stood up and all I could see was him tumbling down, falling beneath the equipment. Being crushed."

She frowned. "That's a glass half-empty if I ever heard it."

A tiny muscle in his jaw twitched slightly. "He's the only thing I have, Lizzie. The thought of anything happening to him makes me a little crazy."

A little? She did a slow count to ten. Only made it to five, but it was enough to keep from smacking him upside the head. For the moment.

She didn't apologize for taking Zeke on the tractor.

She didn't commiserate with the depths of Heath's worry, either.

She understood his words. They pained her, to think how much he thought of his child with Anna, but then, Zeke was real to him. Their tiny boy, Matthew, hadn't existed in Heath's realm. He'd been a fleeting thought.

Not to her.

To her he'd been real. So very real.

She pivoted and walked away before she said too much.

"Liz."

She didn't turn. She refused to turn, because then he'd see the sheen of tears. The quivering jaw.

He hadn't cared then. Pretending to care

now would get them nowhere, so why push him to sympathy?

She kept walking, head high, and if she swiped her hands to her eyes once or twice, he wouldn't know it. Because when she glanced back as she moved through the broad barn door, he was halfway to the house. And he didn't look back.

Chapter Twelve

Alone in a house full of people.

The thought hit Heath when he found Liz on the side porch the next morning. He'd had thirteen hours to consider her words. The truth in them frustrated him.

She'd curled up on the side-porch swing. Her laptop lay perched on her knees and a hot, steaming mug of coffee sat on the rustic wooden table alongside the swing. The cool air lifted the steam like one of those holiday coffee commercials. He didn't ask. Didn't hesitate. He plunked himself down on the end of the swing, and braced his arms on his legs. The action made the laptop teeter.

She reached out to right it. So did he. And this time, when their eyes met, he wanted them to go right on meeting. Like maybe forever. He studied her while she studied him right back, and when he spoke, it was almost like talking with his old friend again. "You're right about Zeke. And about me. And the faith thing you called me out on."

She opened her mouth to speak, but he shook his head. "I've messed up. I've done good things, too, but I'm not afraid to own up to my mistakes. I did wrong by you years ago, and I've never forgiven myself for that. All this time, it's sat there, niggling me, and I wasn't man enough to come to you and say I'm sorry for letting things get out of hand. If I'd been a stronger man, you wouldn't have been put in that position. It was wrong of me, and I apologize, Liz. Please forgive me." He wasn't sure what he wanted her to say, or what he expected, but his action was thwarted by a really cute kid.

"Dad?" Zeke bounded out the side door with all the enthusiasm a new day had to offer. "Miss Corrie said I can carry a special thing for Uncle Sean's ceremony, like a real important thing with his name on it! Isn't that awesome? I've got to practice marching right now!" He flew down the stairs, picked up a stick, and with the stick held high in front of him, he began a solemn march across the gravel, back and forth.

"That's perfect, son." Heath turned back toward Liz.

She wasn't looking at him.

She was watching Zeke as if her heart and soul were bound in his actions. As she watched, a single tear left a pale gleam down her right cheek. "Liz."

He reached over to wipe away the tear.

She didn't let him. She swiped it away herself, and kept her attention on Zeke. "Consider yourself forgiven, Heath. There were two of us involved—"

"I was older…"

She interrupted him swiftly. "Regardless. Plenty of blame to go around. But thank you for your kind words."

She slipped off the swing and tucked the laptop beneath her left arm. "What about Zeke?"

Her quick and almost curt reaction wasn't what he wanted, but it was probably what he deserved. He stood and answered her question. "I'd consider it a real favor if you'd help keep an eye on him with me. He's already told me that he loves Rosie-Posie but he's never going back there because he likes it when his Lizzie takes care of him. So that's going to be an interesting hurdle to handle in a few weeks' time."

"It won't be that huge a hurdle." She indicated the marching boy with a quick glance and a soft smile, a smile that made Heath wish there was room for him in that smile, too. "It's not like I'm going anyplace, so it doesn't have to be a standoff. It can simply be a change of venue."

"How'd you get good at this?" He motioned toward Zeke. "Knowing how to handle kids, how to work with them. It doesn't come naturally to everyone."

"That's easy." She looked at him this time, the trace of tears gone. "I watched Corrie raise Charlotte and Mel. I saw her take them under her wing, two little girls who would have no memory of their mother, and she just helped them blossom into the amazing women they are today. A part of me has always wanted to be like Corrie. Strong. Courageous. Invincible."

"Well, it works. You sure are good with him." He reached out and drew the screen door open for her. "I'm grateful, Liz. When I'm not being a jerk."

She wanted to drink in the scent of him. Soap-and-water fresh, nothing fancy. Cotton, just washed. A few hours into the rising heat of the day and that would change, but for now it heightened her senses.

"How about some breakfast, buddy?" Heath called back to Zeke as he held the door wide.

"With my Lizzie? Yes!" Zeke tossed his stick along the edge of the steps and climbed the stairs quickly. "Cookie said he was making oatmeal, and I don't even like it one little bit, but I think he was teasing because you know what I smell?" He laughed up at them, grabbing a hand from each. "Pancakes! With chocolate chips, I think!"

Zeke's hand gripped hers. Heath was holding his son's other hand, and here they were, joined by a child like they were so many years ago, young lovers, impetuous, not looking down the long road of life.

It shouldn't feel right, but it did, as if the second chance she never thought she'd wanted lay here, right here, in the hills of Western Idaho.

Was she being silly?

One glance toward Heath said maybe not, because he was noting their joined hands, too. And smiling.

"I'm so starvin'!" Zeke pulled them forward, then released their hands. "I'll race you to the kitchen!" He darted off, knowing he wasn't supposed to run in the house, but the pancake-scented air was too much of a draw.

Her hand felt suddenly empty, holding nothing but air, and just as she realized that, Heath's hand covered hers. Clasped it. And then he drew it up gently. "My hand remembers your hand, Lizzie. Like it wasn't all that long ago. Like it's here and now."

He'd asked for forgiveness moments ago. Not for abandoning her, but for creating a child with her. Did he not understand that of the two, being forsaken was far worse than being loved? Maybe to him it hadn't been true love. She'd learned that men often speak of love when what they wanted was a physical relationship. And Heath, for all his wonderful strengths, had given up on faith. That was a deal breaker, right there.

She withdrew her hand gently. "Our here and now is a whole different thing, though, isn't it? We've grown up. Moved on. But for an accident of timing, we would have no idea what the other one was doing at this point. It's good that we still work well together," she went on, but then she hooked a thumb in Zeke's direction. "Over most things." She tucked the computer under one arm and picked up her coffee with the other. "I think I'll catch up on things at the barn. Check and see if our little friend has made a reappearance."

She started to move off, but Heath braced a hand against the wall, blocking her in. "What if the timing isn't accidental?" He didn't give her much space, and right then, gazing up, space was the last thing she wanted. "What if this is our destiny, Liz?"

Liz didn't believe in destiny. She believed in faith, in choices, both good and bad. After a lifetime filled with broken promises, she'd learned that actions spoke way louder than words, and Heath's actions said two things: he'd loved his wife and his beautiful son, and he'd been able to disregard their baby as an inconvenience. So be it.

That might be a maturity thing, or a character flaw, she wasn't sure which, but she was sure of one thing: she never wanted to take a chance on it again. "In a life rife with coincidences, this is simply another one, Heath. Let's not make it more than it is, okay?"

She moved by him, greeted the incoming stockmen with a smile and walked toward the stables.

"So what did you two do today?" Heath broached the question carefully so that Lizzie wouldn't feel like he was checking up on her that night.

Zeke hugged him around the legs and pointed toward the ranch driveway. "We took flowers to Rosie-Posie, we saw baby Jo-Jo and we gave out papers to a lot of people in their mailboxes and we hope we don't get in big, deep trouble. Is that right?" he called to Lizzie across the farmyard driveway.

"That is one hundred percent correct. And we practiced rhyming words and numbers and letter sounds and fishies in the creek and habitats. And mucked stalls and watched for signs of labor and saw none."

"Dad." Zeke reached up to be held and Heath hauled him up, into his arms. He was getting big for this, but Heath wanted to grab every chance he could to show the boy his love. Growth and independence would make this a no-deal soon enough. Too soon, Heath decided as Zeke did that smushy face thing he liked so well. "Did you know that everything has a habitat thing? Like our house and our farm is our habitat thing, and for fish it's a water thing, and for toads it's a shady thing."

Heath tested the boy's understanding with a question. "What does habitat mean?"

"It's where things live, silly!" Zeke crowed that he knew something his father didn't. "So where we can live is our habitat thing! Isn't that so cool? I think God makes it that way on purpose, don't you think so, my Lizzie?"

"Absolutely. He's pretty smart, that God."

"And like when it gets really cold out, I can put on a coat. And some mittens."

"That's adapting. That means you can change your behavior to fit the situation and make the best of it."

"So God made us so we can change!" Zeke bumped knuckles with Heath. "That's like so perfect!"

"It's hard to argue his logic." Heath said the words softly, and when Lizzie leaned forward to rub noses with his son, a longing gaped open inside the father. A longing so deep and wide, he wondered how he hadn't noticed it before.

"It is, therefore I won't argue because Zeke Caufield is an amazingly smart little boy."

Zeke laughed and leaned forward from Heath's arms. He grabbed Lizzie in a hug, and there they were, meshed together, him, Lizzie and Zeke, in a group hug he hadn't sought, but thoroughly enjoyed. "So what were you guys putting in mailboxes, therefore breaking federal law?"

Liz looked downright guilty. "I know we're not supposed to do it, but I couldn't think of another way right now, at least not until I get an email list of neighbors."

"And you need this because…"

"I think the best way of facing the town's troubles is raising awareness and opening the conversation."

"Isn't that what tonight's meeting is for?"

Zeke spotted the growing kittens near the first barn and squirmed to get down. "Dad, I'm gonna go play with the kitties. My Lizzie says it's one of my jobs on the ranch, 'kay?"

"Very okay." He set him down and watched as Zeke raced across the gravel. The kittens were bigger and faster than they were a few weeks prior. And instead of running from the boy, the kittens chased toward him to play. "They're not crazy cats anymore. When did this happen?" he wondered out loud.

"We play with them every day, at least two times, so they won't go feral," Lizzie answered. "And I think Mrs. Hathaway needs a kitten. She mentioned it when we stopped by her place."

Old Mrs. Hathaway was an eccentric and fairly grumpy widow whose husband had governed a big spread of land north of Pine Ridge Ranch. The elderly woman lived in a decaying mansion-styled house a little closer to the Payette National Forest. He didn't know her, but then, he didn't know much of anyone if he didn't see them at church services. And it wasn't like he stayed to talk. Not with so much work to be done.

"She mentioned a mice problem, and I told her we've got kittens here. Would you have a problem with her taking one or two?"

"Anything that cuts down rodent populations is all right by me. How did you run into her?"

"She was getting the mail when we pulled up to leave a flyer about the memorial service. She didn't look well and we helped her back up to the porch."

"Then we took her some food," said Zeke from his spot with the kitties. "She said that was a—" He struggled for the word, then aimed his attention to Lizzie. "What did she say?"

"It was a thoughtful thing to do."

"Oh, yeah!" He grinned. "So that was nice. Wasn't it, Dad?"

"Real nice." He tipped the brim of his cowboy hat up slightly. "Mrs. Hathaway isn't exactly hurting for money as far as I know. She's kind of a recluse…"

"Lot of that going around these hills," said Lizzie, and he couldn't deny it.

"She was hungry? Like for real?"

"I don't think she's healthy enough to cook for herself. Or maybe it's a strength thing, because her appetite was solid. But she's thin and seems lonely."

"I haven't seen her at Sunday services."

"And I don't expect anyone's been checking on her." Sympathy brought her brows together. "That's the worst part of this town decline, Heath. No one's checking on anyone. How sad is that?"

It was sad. Sadder yet was needing Lizzie to point him in the right direction.

"I think I like this little fellow the very best, Dad!"

Zeke's enthusiastic callout broke the moment. "Maybe orange kitties would be best in our barn habitat!"

"Orange rocks." Lizzie started to cross toward the barn as Rosie and Harve walked their way, pushing an old-style buggy, the image of a happy family.

He wanted that, he realized as they drew closer. He hadn't thought of the option in years, but now, with Lizzie on the ranch, making a difference in Zeke's life and his, he didn't just think about it.

He longed for it.

Harve was beaming.

Rosie looked happy. So happy. And when

the baby peeped a tiny sound from the buggy, Lizzie came back their way. "Is this her first walk?" she asked, smiling.

"Her very first." Rosie reached in and lifted the tiny girl. "We wanted to show her the beautiful ranch on which she lives. How blessed we are to be part of all this, to be here, in America. To have this new beginning."

The baby shut her eyes tight against the light. And then she brought one perfect and tiny fist to her mouth in a move he remembered like it was yesterday, from the time he and Zeke had fumbled their way through those first grief-filled months.

"We wanted her first walk to be over here because we wanted to ask you a question." Harve directed his attention to Heath as he laid an arm around Rosie's shoulders. "We would like you to be godfather to Johanna. It would honor us greatly if you would accept this. Sean gave us the opportunity to work here, and you have worked side by side with me and Aldo from the beginning. It would be our pleasure to have you stand with us at her christening."

"Not Aldo?" Heath was pretty sure his voice might have squeaked in surprise because this was a big deal. "Will his feelings be hurt?"

"Aldo is in full agreement," Rosie told him. She adjusted the baby to her shoulder and rocked her gently. "He is Harve Junior's godfather and we would all like you to be a guiding force in our daughter's life. My sister Amina is coming midsummer. She will be Johanna's godmother, so we'll have the service then."

A godparent.

Never had he been asked to do such a thing, nor had he considered it, but he accepted the offer quickly. "I'm the one who's honored," he told them. He thrust out a hand, then gave Harve a half hug instead, thumping him on the back. "I'm so happy for you guys, so yes, I'd love this. Thank you for asking. For thinking of me. Just—" He was blabbering, but he couldn't seem to stop. "Thank you."

"Rosie-Posie, the kitties are nice now? See?" Zeke waved from his spot near the barn. "We're making them nice so they can find happy homes to live in. Isn't that a great idea?"

"It is, my friend." Rosie smiled his way, but kept the newborn away from the kitties and grubby hands. "It is the best of ideas. Yours, I take it." She addressed Lizzie and smiled when she nodded. "It is good for this little man to have new influences in his life.

I regret that our home has been so busy with babies this past year that I have not been able to do things I would like to do with Ezekiel."

"He told me about the twins. That's a lot to handle."

"Their mother has much conflict with the world. With her family. There is no love between Valencia's mother and Valencia, so she is no help with those precious babies." Concern darkened Rosie's eyes. "Valencia speaks of moving away, then staying, then moving. But where she would go, a single mother with two in arms, we do not know." She exchanged a look of worry with Harve. "So we pray. We watch those babies and we pray. For now they are with a friend as I recover. But then, who knows?"

The baby squirmed. She opened her mouth in a soundless cry that would not be soundless for long.

Rosie tucked her back into the buggy. "We shall walk with swifter feet, I think."

Heath watched them go. The sounds of Zeke and the kittens gave a sense of normalcy to an abnormal situation. "I had no idea things were like that. Valencia's situation with her mother."

"There's a lot we don't see when we are so focused on one thing." Lizzie jutted her chin toward the town. "Can it be fixed? Or is it too late? That might be something you and the other bigwigs around here need to ask yourselves."

"I'm not a bigwig," Heath protested, but when she indicated the beautiful spread of Pine Ridge with a quiet look, he rescinded the words. "I'm not some great community leader, Liz. I'm a cowboy who was raised by a drunken father and a mother who disappeared a long time ago. I'm not exactly a model citizen."

"Then you'd better hone your skills, or you'll have no community to speak of. And I don't see that as a great way to raise your son. Do you?"

She walked away, leaving him with more questions than answers while Zeke played nearby.

His son.

Baby Johanna.

Valencia's babies.

What would life be like for these sweet youngsters if everything fell apart around them?

Dude, it's already fallen apart. The question is, can it be put back together? Is there enough left to work with?

As Zeke squealed laughter at kitty antics,

reality hit him square. If the entire town dissolved, could he justify raising his son here? Should he? Was the ranch enough?

That thought sobered him further.

He didn't like spending time going to stupid meetings or blabbing about change. But instead of being a reluctant participant, he'd go to the evening meeting with goals in mind. How to approach the state government to reconsider the grazing rights issue…and how to help the town recover.

Making himself part of the town could be a good first step. He only hoped it wasn't too little, too late.

"Well, go big or stay home," drawled Jace about four hours later. He shot a grin toward Heath. "Committee chairperson? And you said yes?"

"Only because I know I've got letter-writing help on hand," answered Heath. He looked at Liz through the rearview mirror. "If the offer still stands."

"It does. And it was nice to meet all those farmers and ranchers. But almost no one from town, even though these problems have an effect on all of us."

"The town's pretty empty," offered Heath.

Jace turned her way. "The town had more

people living in it when I was growing up here. They've torn down a few old houses and boarded up some others. It could use a facelift, for sure, but with no one to live in the houses, what would be the point?"

"My sister will see the point," said Lizzie. She jotted a note into her phone. "Melonie sees potential in the simplest things. So what aspects of a town do we need? For survival?"

"Jobs." Heath spoke first. "If there are no jobs, there is no survival."

"How do we create jobs out of nothing?" asked Jace.

"Well only the good Lord can do that," answered Lizzie, but she made another note. "Stores. Shops. Services. Church renovation."

"Lack of investment capital," replied Heath. He sounded flat. "Who wants to invest funds in a high-risk venture with little potential?"

"No one," answered Jace, but Lizzie made them think with her next statement.

"You're talking like men."

The two men exchanged blank looks.

"You've got to get to the heart of the matter. If people have reason to love a town, they fight for it. It's not about opportunity only. It's about emotion. Compassion. People helping people."

"Where was she ten years ago?" wondered Jace. "Because we might have had a shot then."

"We've got a shot now," she replied. "You should have seen people's faces when Zeke and I brought the flyer around about Uncle Sean's memorial. If you get to the heart of the matter, you get results. That's all I'm saying."

"It will be a wonderful memorial." Heath met her gaze once more. "And we're grateful that you and Corrie have taken it on. But I don't know how you turn a one-day prayer service into a movement."

"It's real nice of you and Corrie to do this, Lizzie." Jace turned and smiled her way again.

They didn't see the potential.

Lizzie did.

She and Corrie spent the next two weeks working and chatting with people. She supervised two more foals and kept the stray dog's food dish full. On rainy days she tucked it beneath a covered bench to keep the food dry, and by the end of the two weeks, the little dog seemed stronger. Still a mess…but rounder, and less furtive. Corrie proved to be a great emissary and Zeke got to know the layout of the town. The current lambing season was quieting down, in time for haying season to begin as the sun sloped higher in the northern sky.

The last Sunday in May was Reverend Sparks's final day on the pulpit. A subdued group of people filled the church. Before the opening prayer he gazed around the church, from person to person and smiled. "If we'd gotten this kind of turnout more regularly, we'd be staying open!"

Some folks squirmed, but most offered wry smiles, and when he completed the service, he shook hands, one by one, outside. When he got to Lizzie's hand, he held it a little bit longer. "You're beginning to make a difference, Miss Fitzgerald."

"Call me Lizzie."

His smile deepened. "I'll see you tomorrow for the memorial service, and I want to thank you for asking me to officiate. It is an honor to stand tall at a military service. My dad served. And my brother. It means a lot to our family."

He squeezed her hand lightly, and moved on to the next person.

Zeke grabbed her other hand. "Are we baking the cakes today? For real?"

"Cakes and shortcakes because Miss Corrie got a great deal on strawberries."

"I love them so much!"

So did Lizzie. "And you can be our kitchen helper, okay? Although…" She withdrew her phone as her app signaled. "Well, it might be just you and Corrie and Cookie in the kitchen. It looks like we're having foal number five today." Corrie had just joined them and Lizzie held up the app. "I'm abandoning the kitchen in favor of the foaling stall."

Corrie accepted that like she accepted most anything. "No matter. Rosie is cooking, and Cookie and I can handle everything else with the help of our young friend here."

"And I'm making the cupcakes. Right? Because being a kitchen helper is a real important job."

"That it is," Corrie told him.

Mrs. Hathaway came their way and put out a hand to Corrie. "I don't believe I know you."

"I don't believe you do." Corrie took the old woman's hand gently. "Corrie Satterly. I'm helping out at Pine Ridge Ranch."

"Are you the cleaning lady?" Mrs. Hathaway asked.

Lizzie's cheeks went red. She was pretty sure her mouth dropped open and she was just about to leap to Corrie's defense, when Corrie laughed and tucked the old woman's arm through hers. "I do my share of that, for certain." She smiled and the old woman smiled, too. Kind of. "I help out with this and that and you know how it is with a barn full of men. They are always needing something, aren't they?"

"I expect there's truth in that." Mrs. Hathaway motioned to her car. "Do you mind walking an old woman over? My feet don't like to listen to my head the way they used to."

Corrie walked her over as Heath crossed the churchyard for Zeke. "I've never seen Gilda Hathaway in church. Or talking to people."

"She thought Corrie was our cleaning woman, Heath."

He winced. "Sean used to call Gilda an old bat. She didn't have a kind word to say about anything or anyone and holed herself up in that great old house and let it dissolve around her. He offered to buy some of her land and she offered to call the sheriff, so he wasn't too pleased with her. Having her come down to the service is about as out of character as you can get. Call me if you need help in the horse barn."

"You're cutting hay today."

"All this week. Watching the forecast and hoping nothing breaks down." He walked her to her SUV. "It was nice to have the reverend bless the farmers and ranchers. To hear him talk about the everyday people. The simple folk."

"Jesus didn't recruit prominent men to do his work, Heath." She leaned back against the car and gazed up at him. "Fishermen. Tradesmen. A tax collector, a repugnant profession even then." She smiled at his expression of agreement. "His father was a carpenter. His friends and followers worked with their hands. When you talk about not being a community leader, you're wrong. You're exactly the type of leader Shepherd's Crossing needs. I'm just hoping you'll turn out to be one of many."

"It's not a one-man job, that's for sure."

"Which is why we reach out to others." She opened her car door. "It's a start."

"It is." He glanced around at the number of people still there, saying their goodbyes to the pastor. "Because I've never seen this many people darken the doors of this church. Not even on Christmas and Easter."

"Sometimes the greatest good comes out of the worst circumstance. See you at home."

At home.

He watched her pull away and realized what he wanted. What he needed.

He needed her. He needed her by his side, keeping him focused, keeping him grounded.

He'd loved her as a young man. Watching her car pull away, he realized he loved her now, too.

The aged pastor was still shaking hands.

His gentle words of blessing had touched Heath's heart.

He thought about that as Zeke scrambled into his car seat in the truck and fastened his seat belt.

Was there a God for real? Did He exist? Did He have a heart for humankind, the way the pastor said? Or was it all silly feel-good talk to keep people in line, like the easygoing sheep, one plodding after the other, rarely thinking for themselves?

He didn't know, but seeing the light of faith in Lizzie's eyes and Corrie's bearing, for the first time in a long time, he wanted to know.

"Dad. I'm so 'cited about today, I'm so 'cited to be a kitchen helper with Miss Corrie and my Lizzie!" Tangible joy lit Zeke's face. "And then I get to march with my plaque thing tomorrow! I will be the best marcher, ever, Dad. The best!"

"I know you will, son." He aimed a smile at his beautiful boy through the rearview mirror. "And I can't wait to see it."

"Me, either!" The boy wriggled with all the anticipation of youth. "And my Lizzie will be so proud of me." He grinned again, and Heath saw what was missing. What had been missing, for so long.

He'd grown up without a mother, and that emptiness had left a gaping hole in so much of what he did. Zeke had no memories of a mother, of that softer side of encouragement. The warmth. The glee.

And Lizzie had grown up the same way, her mother gone far too soon. But she'd had Corrie's love and devotion. The strength and wisdom of a good woman, guiding all three girls along the way.

Better than anyone, Lizzie would be able to lovingly accept his son as her own.

His thumb went to his empty ring finger, and this time it didn't feel naked. It felt right, like it was supposed to be that way.

Anna would want him to move on. He knew that. She'd want what was best for their son and for him, and what was best for them was Lizzie. Now he needed to do whatever it took to convince the lady in question.

She wanted faith, hope and love. His job was to make sure she got all three.

Chapter Thirteen

A small army of vehicles snaked their way up the Pine Ridge Ranch drive Memorial Day morning. Car after car worked their way toward the barnyard, then parked along the barn's edges as if finding a spot along a small-town street. As the minutes ticked closer to ten o'clock, the yard and the graveled drive filled with people. More people than Heath thought lived in a five-mile radius.

"About time someone's doing something to remember this man." Gilda Hathaway came forward. She'd looked unhappy when he first met her a dozen years before. She looked just as unhappy now. "I had my differences with Sean Fitzgerald, but then I've had my differences with most everyone. Where will this begin? Here?" She indicated the grassy slope. "In the house?" She swept the steps a fierce look, then brought it back to Heath. "In the barn?"

There was no time to reply because a somewhat hunched older gentleman offered his hearty hello as he came up beside her.

"I met Sean some thirty years back," he said, after greeting Gilda and Heath. "That was when he first come to these parts, and while I'm sorry the men in the hills can't be here, I wanted to come and pay my respects." His voice rasped as if short on air, but his eyes gleamed with gentle wisdom. "Sean wanted this place to sit up and take notice, and we won't ever forget that. Not all wanted to listen and he wasn't a time waster."

Heath understood the truth in that. Sean valued time and industry.

"He gave out his share of good advice, too," the old fellow continued, "and I wasn't afraid or too proud to take it." He offered a gnarled, arthritic hand to Heath. Would it hurt the old-timer to shake his hand? Heath had no idea. Using a gentle touch, he accepted the hand with care.

"Name's Boone Webster," the aged man told him. Shocks of gray hair peeked out from beneath a cowboy hat that had seen better days two decades back. "I spent my share of time on a lot of farms and ranches in my day. When my hands worked."

"Boone's old but he makes a mean pot of venison stew," Gilda announced to anyone who would listen, and by that time, there were a few dozen folks closing in on them. She didn't break a smile, but she seemed almost approving, and Heath was pretty sure the old-timer blushed. "He's got a heart for doin' good, for all the good that's done him."

"Now, Gilda. You said you wouldn't fuss today," Boone reminded her in a gentler tone than she probably deserved. "Today we're respecting the dead and rejoicing the living. Remember?" He nodded across the yard and the old woman followed his look to a group of locals. Ben, Jace, Aldo and a few other ranch hands rounded out the group.

"I remember, all right."

"Well, good."

"Glad to be here, Heath!" called one woman as Gilda and Boone moved on.

"Harve, good to see you! Congratulations on your new daughter!" Blake Melos's younger sister had spotted Harve and Rosina coming their way.

Seven old men came in military uniform. Three of them unfurled flags, and three others carried long guns.

Folks were greeting one another all around him, like a potluck gathering, and when Eric Carrington and two of the other big landowners joined the group, Heath saw the brilliance in the moment. Lizzie's brilliance.

He turned as she and Corrie approached the porch stairs. "You reached out to all these people to put this together."

"Zeke and I informed people of the date and time, with a message about Sean's service and his love for Idaho. Their hearts did the rest."

"Theirs and yours." Gazing down, he glimpsed what the future could be like with this woman. He'd known it a dozen years before, but he'd been too young to understand the full implications.

Now he did. Lizzie didn't back down. She never gave up. She moved forward, saying what she meant, and meaning what she said.

"Are you the gal who put this in my mailbox?" A middle-aged woman came close.

Lizzie met her with a welcoming smile. "Guilty as charged."

"Well, it was like old times, walkin' out there and findin' somethin' to read again," the woman declared. "Like when the weekly arrived in the old days. I'd grab that up and read it front to back to see what was going on, especially in the winter. During rough snows it was about the only way to stay in contact with people before the snow plows got commissioned. I forgot how much I missed that until I found that paper in my box. And so well-written, too!"

Lizzie's smile grew. "I do love writing," she confessed to the woman. "And every little town could use its own paper, couldn't it?"

"Just to see what's what," the woman agreed. "Nothin' too big or fancy. Just enough."

Lizzie moved to the top step. She raised a hand, and when folks noticed, they got quiet. Zeke had slipped out the side door. When he spotted Lizzie, he moved her way and tucked himself beneath her left arm, close to her heart...and she snugged that arm right around him in welcome, confirming what Heath had figured out.

She belonged here. With him. With his son. In Heath's arms, day and night. Now his job would be to convince her of that.

"We want to thank you for coming today." She smiled at the gathering of people and they smiled right back. "I didn't know my uncle Sean, but the memories you emailed to us painted a picture of a wonderful man who left us too soon. While Uncle Sean wanted his ashes sprinkled on the land he loved so well, we decided that there should be a place to remember him." She pointed to a spot between the house and the road. "He liked shade, so we picked a favorite group of trees. He liked sun, so the garden faces south-west. He was born a Southerner, and while Southern plants don't transplant well to Idaho, woodcrafts do, so the benches in the garden are from Kentucky. But more than anything, my uncle Sean loved God and his country. He loved Idaho. The beauty of the valley and the majesty of the mountains. We see it here in his house. On this ranch. And in the kind of job he did every single day. From the bat-tlefield where he risked his life to save oth-ers and here, where he opened the doors of opportunity to others." She smiled at Harve, Rosie and Aldo, then gave a slight pause be-fore she went on. "Anger and division kept our family at odds a long time. Our hope is that this memorial today, on a day when we remember those who've served our country, becomes one that brings family, friends and this sweet town back together." She looked down. "Zeke. Are you ready?"

His son nodded and Lizzie handed him the plaque to carry.

The elderly honor guard took their places.

Flags in hand, guns shouldered, they began the solemn walk to the driveway's curve.

When they got to the curve they veered left, toward a small copse of trees. There was no casket flag to fold. There were no ashes to scatter. But as they set the flags into newly installed flag holders, the freshly landscaped site took on a new meaning.

It wasn't the patch of flowers the women had tucked in front of a few trees.

It wasn't the two rustic benches inviting quiet repose.

With the flags in place, and a single bagpiper standing by while seven old fellows stood at attention, Heath began to see new possibilities out of old realities.

Reverend Sparks was there to lead them in prayer, but he'd asked Heath to say a few words in remembrance, enough to remind people who Sean was. What he meant to him, Ben, Aldo and Harve. To Jace and Wick. To so many.

He shifted slightly to the right and faced the crowd. "I'm keeping this short, like Sean liked," he promised. That garnered a few smiles. "But also to the point, because Sean respected that, too.

"Sean Fitzgerald was a good man. He took care of his own, and he reached out to find the best folks to do the job to make his dream come true. When you look around Pine Ridge, you can see he did exactly that. But he wanted more," Heath told the people. He met a few looks of surprise, then adjusted his meaning. "Not for himself. For the town. The people in it. He ran out of time, and he'd be the first to admit he might have back-burnered it too long. Today, I'd like to see that change." He met the eyes of Eric Carrington and two other wealthy landowners who were rarely seen around town. "Big spreads are nice, but if we don't work together to save this town, *our town*—" he stressed the words gently "—we could regret it. I think most of us have had enough regrets in our lives. Something to think on, anyway, while we pray together."

He linked hands with Lizzie on one side and Zeke on the other, and when the aged pastor led them in prayer, a flicker of hope began within him. Not a big, burning flame. Nothing so grandiose. Just enough to recall Lizzie's words, how everything had to begin somewhere.

Three old soldiers stepped forward. Aiming high, they shot seven volleys into the clear blue sky, marking the moment.

He hadn't had a lot of time to mourn when

Anna died. There was too much to do, and Zeke did enough crying for both of them.

And he'd held back tears during Sean's final days and his passing because Sean had entrusted him with a huge job. Tears had no place at such moments. He didn't want his dear friend and mentor to spend his last earthly moments worrying about the ranch.

But today, tears slipped down his cheeks.

Not too many, and he dashed them away, but enough to know that maybe he'd grown a bigger, better heart somewhere along the way.

Lizzie hadn't known Sean, but she clutched a wad of tissues to swipe tears away as she watched the solemn military salute.

And then one lone bagpiper stepped forward to play "Amazing Grace."

The poignant notes of the familiar tune... with the row of aged men standing at attention, their love for God and country so obvious...

His throat choked up all over again.

Then Lizzie left him no choice. She leaned her head against his arm. He put his left arm around her shoulders and pulled her closer, then leaned down to kiss her forehead.

He didn't care if people saw.

He didn't care what some might think.

He thought of what she'd missed all her

life, the love and care of parents who cherished her.

Could she be happy here?

She lifted watery eyes to his and the moment she did, he knew his answer.

Yes.

She could love him again. Would love him again. It was written in her heartfelt gaze, through the sheen of sorrow.

Zeke tugged on his sleeve. He looked down into a little face lined with worry. Zeke reached up and Heath scooped him into his arms.

He held him in one arm and Lizzie in the other, and for the first time in a long time, Heath was pretty sure everything was going to be all right.

Lizzie had just finished up in the stables when Heath came her way a few hours later. "Has everyone gone home?"

He nodded. "Even the few old timers that hung around, just wanting to chat. Wick drove the last couple home. And Lizzie..." He moved closer, and his look...

Lizzie was pretty sure she could get lost in that look if they shared all three blessings. Faith, hope and love.

"I wanted to thank you."

He laid strong hands on her shoulders in a gentle grip and held her gaze. "You saw what needed to be done and you did it. You reached out and people responded. Having this service today made a difference. It brought people together that I haven't seen in years."

"Let's not get carried away," she began, but he paused her with a finger to her mouth. "Why not?"

Her heart began to beat harder. Faster.

He stepped closer. "Maybe just a little carried away." He smiled down at her as his eyes went from her eyes to her lips…and back again. "Like this." He leaned down and paused just shy of her mouth, waiting for her to close the distance.

Lizzie didn't make him wait. She rose up on tiptoe to touch her mouth to his, and when he gathered her into his arms, a rush of sweet emotion grabbed hold.

She'd loved him once. Probably never stopped. And now…

"Liz." He pressed kisses to her cheek, her ear, her hair. "You've made a difference, Lizzie. Not just to me, but to my son, to this ranch, and maybe to the town." He stopped talking long enough to kiss her again. Then he paused and dropped his forehead to hers. "I can't let you go again, Liz. Not now, not ever. I want you to stay here, with me. With Zeke. I want us to be a family, Liz. I want to court you like I should have done years ago."

She started to speak but stopped when a long, drawn-out whine pierced the air.

They both paused, listening.

The whine came again, fainter this time.

"The dog." Lizzie pulled back and raced for the door. Heath followed.

She didn't burst through the back door. She opened it carefully, not wanting to scare the animal. She crept out, with Heath behind her, and searched the pasture with her eyes.

The yowl came again, long and slow as if begging for help.

And then the dog appeared at the edge of the shed. She started their way, then paused, panting.

They navigated over the split rail fence and ran toward the dog. Normally it would have ducked away into hiding.

Not this time. This time the roughed-up pooch stayed right there, waiting.

Lizzie moved right in. Heath caught her arm. "An animal in pain might bite. Let me get her."

Lizzie pulled off the hoodie she'd had tied around her waist. "Wrap her in this. She's shaking, Heath."

He bent over the dog, wrapped her in the soft jacket and lifted her into his arms as if he carried something precious and beautiful. Not a sad, dirty, matted canine. "Let's get her up to the house."

"Not the barn?"

He shook his head quickly. "I think she's going to need some warmth and TLC, Lizzie. She's very pregnant and seems to be going into labor."

"She's having puppies?"

He nodded, grim. "Let's see if we can get her cleaned up some. There might not be time for that, though."

She moved up the steps ahead of him as his phone alarm went off. The dog jumped in his arms, frightened by the sudden noise. He held her close while Lizzie drew a bath in the laundry room sink.

His phone buzzed again. He frowned, hit Decline, and helped hold the weak dog as Lizzie sluiced warm water through the nasty fur. When the dog let out a yelp, Lizzie put the hand sprayer down. "Let's let her rest now. We got the worst of it. Are there flea meds in the barn?"

"Yes. Good thought. Cookie would not approve of fleas in his work area. I'll have one of the men bring them in." He held up his phone in apology. "The meeting that Carrington scheduled is today. It's in fifteen minutes. I don't know how long I'll be, but I know he's got an early flight back to the East Coast." He looked from her to the dog and back. "I don't want to leave you with this, but I don't want to miss this chance to talk with these guys, either."

"Strike while the iron's hot," she told him. "You go and figure out what can be done to help the town and—"

The back screen door slapped shut and Zeke barreled their way. He skidded to a stop and plugged his nose. "Something is really smelly around here." He looked from his father to Lizzie, then spotted the wet dog. He moved closer, intrigued, but didn't let go of his nose. "That is a weird dog, my Lizzie."

"A sick dog," said Heath. He bent low. "I don't want you to go near her, okay? We think she's going to have babies."

"Puppies?" His voice pitched up. His eyebrows did, too. "In the house? We never have puppies in the house. I can't even believe that we're going to have puppies in the house."

Cookie had followed him through the door and when he cleared his throat with meaning, Lizzie was pretty sure he couldn't believe it, either. She put a finger to her lips and indicated the worn-out dog with a look.

Zeke clapped a hand over his mouth. "I forgot to use my inside voice." He made a face of regret. "Maybe we should just whisper around the doggie, right? Like this." He whispered so softly that Lizzie didn't have a clue what he was saying.

"I think just a soft voice works. We want her to get used to our voices, so she's not afraid to come into the house."

"Can we keep the puppies? Like here, with us and we can have a dog just for me?" Hopeful, he peered up at his father, but Heath shook his head.

"Zeke, I can't answer that right now. I don't know how this will all turn out. She's not healthy. She's been neglected a long time, so things might not go okay with the puppies. Let's wait and see, okay?"

Zeke's lower lip stuck out. "'Cept when you say wait and see it means no, Dad. It always just means no." He folded his arms and stood stubborn as a mule in a stare-down with his father. "I don't know why I can't have one animal for me when you have like a gazillion all over the place."

Heath's phone buzzed once more. He made a wry face and put the phone away. "On that note…" He bent and kissed Zeke's forehead. "Be good. We'll discuss this later. I've got a meeting to go to. If it's all right with Lizzie, you can help with the dog, but you've got to keep your voice soft, okay? This dog isn't used to people and she sure isn't accustomed to busy little boys." He aimed a look at Lizzie, over Zeke's head. "I'll be back as quick as I can."

"Corrie's on her way back from Rosie's place. Her calm head in a crazy storm mentality is just what we need right now." She dropped her gaze to Zeke and Heath seemed to catch her meaning.

He nodded and left quickly.

"Can I pet her?"

Lizzie shook her head. "Not just yet. She might get nippy. But there is one very important, maybe most important thing you can do, Zeke."

His frown had deepened substantially as she spoke, but it disappeared when she said, "You can name this dog. How can we take care of a little mama dog with no name?"

He grinned, elated with this new assignment. "I don't even know what names to think of!" He kept his voice toned down and his smile in place, but he'd had a long day already and Lizzie knew that could change.

"Well, it's a girl, so we need a girl's name."

"Not Clifford."

She shook her head, because reading about the big red dog's antics was one of Zeke's favorite pastimes. "Definitely a boy's name. Let's go through the alphabet," she suggested. "Addie. Abby. Bria. Belle. Betsy."

"That's it!" Zeke whispered up to her, excited. "Betsy! I think it's the best name ever for a dog that's not so big, right? A name all her own."

Oh, Zeke…

So precious.

So sweet.

And needing a mother to love him. To laugh with him. Challenge him. The thought of that shared kiss didn't just sweep over her. It enveloped her, like a warm blanket on a chilled night.

Zeke yawned once, then yawned again. "I really wish I could just have a dog all my own. I would share him with you." He looked up at Lizzie. "I wouldn't hog him all by myself. But I could play with him a lot. He would be my friend."

Lizzie knew what he meant. The farm had several working dogs, but they weren't allowed to follow a little guy around and go on boy adventures, and there were no children around to play with. "I didn't have a dog, either. We'll talk to your dad later, okay? First, we have to make sure the puppies arrive and that they're all right."

"He'll say no. He says no to everything." Zeke stood, scowled and yawned again, clearly worn with the busy day. And when he got tired, he got grumpy.

"Why don't you take a rest," she suggested softly. "If the puppies start arriving, I'll come get you, okay?"

"I'm not even a little bit tired." He yawned again, punctuating the declaration.

She hid a smile. "You don't have to sleep, darling. Maybe just a rest and a cookie."

"All my favorite cookies are gone." He sighed as if the world had just crumbled around him. "Maybe I'll get one anyway."

"Okay."

She heard him in the kitchen, then the nearby bathroom. She stroked the dog's head, murmuring sweet words of comfort, right up until she heard the scream followed by a solid thud.

Her heart stopped, but the adrenaline punch pumped it right into high gear. As she burst through the door onto the side porch, her heart ground to a halt again because there was Zeke, the beloved boy, lying on the ground.

And he wasn't moving.

Chapter Fourteen

While one volunteer EMT cared for Zeke, a second one addressed the gathered crew of Pine Ridge Ranch. "We've called for the chopper," he explained. "We want him at a level-one trauma hospital, just in case he needs additional services."

"Additional services?" Lizzie gripped his arm. "What does that mean?"

"It's concussion protocol. Some are worse than others and having skilled hands and equipment on hand is clutch. I hear it coming." He pointed south as the sound of the chopper grew. "Let's get him transported and they'll take it from there. With a head trauma like this, we don't want to waste time."

Head trauma.

Zeke.

Lizzie's hands shook. Her fingertips buzzed.

"How far up the tree was he?" the medic asked, and Lizzie had to shake her head.

"I don't know. I was inside and he was going to take a rest. I heard the scream as he fell. I—"

Her voice was lost in the growing noise as the chopper descended into the fresh-cut hayfield nearby. Medics hurried their way, lugging necessary equipment at a dead run.

How had this happened in the space of a few short minutes?

"Zeke." Heath sank to the ground on the other side of the inert child. Anguish darkened his face while worry clouded his eyes.

She hadn't heard him arrive. The sound of his Jeep had been shrouded by the chopper noise.

The first EMT made way for the new arrivals. She approached Heath. "We've got concussion symptoms, Heath. Possibly a broken wrist. They're going to fly him to Boise."

"Am I going to lose him?"

Heath's voice held more than fear. It held the stark reality of life and death. Guilt and sorrow fought for dominance within Lizzie.

"Kids get concussions all the time," she told him. "But he needs care and observation, all of which they can give him. There's so little up here to work with."

They'd immobilized Zeke's little body on some kind of a board.

The sight of the child, lying still and quiet against the hard surface, shattered Lizzie's heart again. He should be kicking and screaming at the thought of being trussed up, but he wasn't.

He couldn't because she'd been too distracted to watch him properly.

"You'll have to drive to the hospital, Heath. There's no room in the chopper. I already checked. Are you okay to drive?"

Of course he wasn't.

Tears filled his eyes. Worry darkened his face. The guy was totally over the top and it was one hundred percent her fault.

"I can drive." She reached for his keys, determined. She'd messed up. It was her job to see it through.

"I'll drive myself."

Lizzie started to protest, but Heath was already moving away. She chased after him. "Let me drive. You're in no condition to—"

"Tell everyone I'll call to let them know what's going on."

He started the engine, turned the car around, and was heading down the driveway as the rescue chopper roared back to life.

And then they were gone, the beat of the

chopper blades leaving a dull thudding noise as the copter headed south.

She stared after the chopper, then Heath's car, then the helicopter again as it faded from sight.

She couldn't stay here, waiting. Heath might not want her with him, but she couldn't stay hours away while that blessed child fought for his life.

"Corrie." She turned as Corrie came up next to her. "I've got to go."

Corrie didn't pretend to hide her concern. "I know, Lizzie-Beth. I know. But do you think it's best, darlin'?"

"Twelve years ago I lay in a strange room, in a strange hospital, all alone while my baby passed away. I can't risk Heath being alone right now. He's got every reason in the world to hate me for risking his son," she admitted, "but I can't leave him there alone. I've got to go to the hospital, Corrie."

"Then we go." Corrie turned toward the house to collect what she'd need.

Lizzie jutted her chin toward the house. "The dog. Betsy. We can't leave her alone."

"I'd forgotten."

Lizzie hurried into the house to retrieve her keys and purse. "You stay here. Stay with her, okay?"

"But…"

"Please?" She grabbed her keys and tucked her purse over her arm. "Don't leave her to have those babies alone. Okay?"

"You'll be all right?" Concern shaded Corrie's tone, but understanding shone in her eyes.

"I will." Lizzie started the engine, then faced her sweet mentor. "Because I have to be."

"We will be praying for all. Drive safely."

"I will."

She turned south on the two-lane, determined. Heath might hate her for this tragic accident. She would deal with that as needed. But she understood the grief of facing loss all alone. No way was she about to let Heath… her hard-working, imperfect beloved…endure the same thing.

Zeke.

Heath's heart pounded as he hurried through the ER doors. He sprinted to the desk, gave Zeke's name, and raced down the hall once he had directions.

"And you are?" A middle-aged woman blocked his way to Zeke's curtained cubicle.

"His father. Are you his nurse?"

The woman pierced him with a look before she sighed, pretending offense. "I'm his doctor. You did well sending him by chopper even though it's a pricey form of taxi. We did a quick scan and see nothing really bad."

"But he's unconscious, isn't he?"

She drew the curtain back so Heath could see. "Sleeping now. And he might sleep all day. It's the brain's defense against injury so the body can concentrate on healing. He's got a broken wrist that we've splinted," she explained softly as she moved into the small, curtained room. "You'll need to have him see an orthopedic doctor in about three days. Do you have an ortho near your home?"

They had next to nothing near the ranch, he realized anew.

What if Zeke had died because there was no medical help nearby?

She must have mistaken his hesitation for confusion because she made a quick note before looking up again. "Never mind, I'll give you a few names. You might have to travel an hour or so but if there's ice cream involved at the end of the trip, it's not so bad. All in all I'd say he's a pretty fortunate boy."

"How is falling from a tree considered fortunate?"

She brushed that off as she wrote something else in a hand-held computer. "Having trees to climb. Places to explore. Things to do. These days too many kids are inside, playing on devices. Boys and girls should have adventurous spirits, shouldn't they? Unless we want to raise them in a bubble."

He stared at her, then Zeke. "Right now the bubble sounds good," he admitted and the doctor laughed.

"I bet it does, but this will give him stories to tell later on. It does bear caution, though. Once a kid has had a concussion, the likelihood for another one is elevated. Just keep that in mind, but don't curtail his curiosity because of it. I'll be back in a little while, but so far, so good. There's a very uncomfortable chair right here." She pointed to it and made a face. "Unfortunately that's all we've got available. The nurses will keep checking in."

"I don't care about the chair. As long as he's going to be all right, I'm fine."

The doctor left. Five minutes later, the curtain opened again. He looked up, expecting to see a nurse, but it wasn't a nurse.

It was Lizzie.

She stood at the curtain's edge, watching Zeke, then winced when Zeke winced. "How is he?"

"The doctor said he's going to be fine. But he might be sleeping here for hours." He stood up and crossed to her. "Did you drive here on your own?"

"Like you did. Yes."

Because he'd been too crazed to have her drive along. What was the matter with him? "I should have just brought you with me," he told her. "I wasn't thinking. All I could think of was that chopper, whisking my boy away and no one would be here to greet him. None of his family, that is. So I rushed away, but we should have come together. I'm sorry."

"It's all right." But it wasn't all right, because it was her responsibility to watch the little guy and she'd failed. Failed miserably. "As long as he's going to be okay. Are you sure about that?" If she felt as guilt-stricken as she looked, she was feeling really bad right now, and that wasn't fair.

"Doctor's words," he assured her. "The EMT was right about the broken wrist. It will put a dent in his summer activities, but it's fixable."

"Good. Good." She reached out a hand to Zeke's shoulder. Tears filled her eyes, and a few slipped over.

"Liz."

"I'm fine, really." She sniffled and he grabbed a few tissues from a small box and thrust them her way. "You know what they say. It's all right to cry after the emergency. Not during."

"You've never been much of a crier, Liz. Ever."

"Well, there's some truth in that. I suppose it depends on the situation," she finished as she swiped her cheeks. "This guy's worth a few tears."

"Aren't all kids?"

This time she raised her head. She stared at him as if he'd grown two heads. A flash of anger, or maybe disappointment, changed her expression, and then she faced him, dead-on. "Yes, Heath. All kids should be loved, cherished, cared for and mourned. Regardless of the circumstances surrounding them."

"Lizzie—" He started to move her way, confused, but she held up a hand. He stopped.

"Don't 'Lizzie' me. Where were you twelve years ago when your first son passed away? Where were you when I was in that wretched little hospital, trying to save Matthew's life, and failed? Where were you when I begged for help, for you to come and stand by me as I miscarried? Because I understand your love for Zeke, Heath. I really do. But where was this love when our tiny baby died? Because I sure could have used a dose of it back then."

Her words shell-shocked him.

He stared at her, unable to digest and believe what he was hearing. "You didn't end our pregnancy on purpose?"

She recoiled as if slapped, then started to move away.

He stepped in her way. "Liz, talk to me. Please. I had no idea that you didn't end the pregnancy. Your father and grandfather told me they'd sent you off to have it terminated so you wouldn't mess up your freshman year at Yale."

"And you believed them?"

He hadn't thought she could look more disappointed and disillusioned, but he was wrong. So wrong, because the minute she said the words, he realized the truth. Lizzie— his Lizzie—wouldn't have done such a thing, so why had he believed their lies? Because he was guilt-stricken over what happened?

He'd figure that out later. Right now he needed to talk to her. Sort this out. Beg forgiveness. "There was no way to get in touch with you. I tried. They'd taken your phone and no one would give me any information. Including Corrie. When Sean called me and offered me a job up here, I came north to start a new life. Liz, I'm sorry. So dreadfully, horribly sorry. I don't even know what to say to you right now to make this better because I can't make it better."

He looked penitent. And sad. Concern drew his brows together, and he looked as if he really cared, but she knew better. "I called you. When things went bad, I called you, over and over. You didn't answer and you didn't return my messages. I faced losing that baby, *our* baby, all by myself, and I lost a part of myself with him. No." She stepped back when Heath made a move to embrace her. "Don't touch me. I thought I knew you, Heath."

"Lizzie, you did. You do." He kept his voice soft to match hers as Zeke slept on.

"The young man I fell in love with would never have believed I could do such a thing. He would never accept the idea that I would terminate a life."

He started to move forward again, but she slipped to the side, and out of the cubicle.

She wouldn't let him see her break down.

She wouldn't let him have the chance to offer words of comfort now because she'd needed them *then*. She'd needed them so badly that her heart broke for lack of it.

She crossed the ER, then the parking lot, then climbed into her car.

She'd meant to stay with him while Zeke mended, but she couldn't. Not now.

He probably thought his excuse was understandable, but it wasn't. Weeks had passed from when she was sent away to when the pregnancy failed. He could have—

She steered toward the road as her conscience kicked into high gear.

Could have what? He was thrown out with nothing but the clothes he had. Where would he be now if Sean hadn't offered him help? And how did Sean know to offer that help?

Corrie.

She drove back toward the ranch, and used the two-hour drive to frame the questions she had for Corrie, starting with how Heath had gotten his job at Pine Ridge Ranch…

And why Corrie had kept it a secret all these years.

Chapter Fifteen

Corrie was on the side porch when Lizzie parked her SUV alongside the house. She exited the car, slammed the door and pounded up the steps. She faced Corrie, the only mother figure she'd known for over twenty-five years, and threw down the gauntlet. "You knew Heath was here all along, didn't you?"

Corrie faced her from the wide-seated rocker. She studied Lizzie for a long, slow moment, then nodded. "I asked Sean to give him a chance. I told him what happened and how your father and grandfather had thrown him out with nothing. No paycheck, no chance to gather things, no chance to say goodbye to you. Absolutely nothing, all because he had the audacity to fall in love with you. That's the kind of men they were, and

258 Her Cowboy Reunion

Heath's own father wasn't one bit better." She sighed and folded her hands into her lap.

"Sean was different. He'd always been different. He took the money he'd inherited and invested it. Then he spent years working the land, working here, to build something unique. Something so far away from publishing that the wheeling and dealing of Fitzgerald News Company couldn't touch him. I figured if Heath had a chance to see what a real man stands for, it would be good for him. And it would give you a chance to grow up a little."

She'd made these decisions without telling Liz. Without giving her a choice. Pressure-cooker anger built inside her. "You never told me. And you never told him about Matthew. He thought I terminated the pregnancy on purpose."

Corrie didn't back down and didn't look one bit guilty. "Isn't that a thing in itself? That he'd believe lies like that back then? Because he shouldn't have believed them, Lizzie. I expect he knows that now."

"You could have told me where he was."

Corrie frowned. "I could have. But to what end? He needed to grow up. He needed to see what a good man does, how a good man stands by his family in thick and thin. You were giving Matthew up for adoption, you'd made that decision and it was a noble one. And then circumstances took it all out of our hands when that tiny fellow went home to God. And there isn't a day that goes by that I don't imagine sitting in heaven one day, rockin' that boy and telling him what a wonderful mother and father he had. Just in case he doesn't know it. I'll share Beulah Land with him and your sweet mama. May God forgive me my mistakes, but then the good Lord knows the reasons for them. And that's for certain."

"I needed him, Corrie," she pressed. "When that baby passed from me, I needed Heath there. With me. By my side. And you thwarted that." She couldn't believe the words as she said them, that her beloved Corrie, the woman who'd loved her all along, who'd come to her side when called, didn't tell her where Heath was.

Corrie stood and faced her. Regret and unshed tears marked her face. "You'd called him. You'd called him over and over and he didn't come. He didn't call back. And you were in such anguish and pain that I had to decide what was best for you. I couldn't help baby Matthew. And I'd done what I thought best and helpful for Heath, by having Sean offer him a job, but when he didn't have the courtesy to answer your phone calls or return your messages, I got angry. Angry at him for not making himself available the way he should have. Angry at him for putting you in that situation. From that day on I never contacted Sean or checked on Heath until we drove up this driveway. And that's the truth of the matter."

She stood strong and solid, a woman of compassion and commitment, a woman who'd stood by the three daughters in her care no matter what.

But the thought that one phone call might have changed everything soured Lizzie's heart. She turned and went down the stairs. She crossed the yard, entered the first barn and brought Honey's Money into the prep area.

She saddled her with quick hands and no mind to where she'd go or what she'd do. Just mind enough to know that she thought better on horseback.

She led the horse into the yard.

Corrie was no longer on the porch. No one was about.

No matter.

She climbed into the saddle and let the horse walk an easy pace toward the ridge.

Once they were in the mowed field, she let the mare have her head and they ran. They ran across the freshly mowed hay lot, across the lower ridge, wide and flat, until the ridge dipped down. She slowed the horse and followed the descent until she found herself in the middle of the failing town.

The old pastor was just leaving the church. He saw her on horseback and stared, surprised. Then he chuckled low and waved her over.

What choice did she have?

The last thing she wanted to do was talk to anyone, and yet the path had brought her here, into the center of town. She dismounted, caught the reins, and walked his way. "I didn't mean to startle you."

"It was a start, for sure," the old man laughed. "I haven't seen anyone ride a horse into town in years, and then it was scarce enough. There are hitching posts right over there. You see 'em?"

She turned and noticed the trio of posts up the road apiece. "An odd place for them, isn't it?"

"Not odd, considering the post office and general store used to stand right there. The Middletons have pictures of it, nothing all that grand, but solid like they used to build them.

And Western-looking with a wide porch, all covered so the lady shoppers would be all right while the farmer husbands had to load grain from the back in the rain, snow and sun. They did right by the ladies, wantin' to take care of them first in those days. It's a cowboy way, and a good one."

He held a set of boxes in his hands. She tied Honey's Money to the hitching post and put out her hands. "May I help you, Reverend?"

"I won't say no," he told her. "I'm heading back to my place." He motioned north. "Standin' in one place bothers my hip. Once it's in motion, it's right enough, but standin' still makes it act up."

"I don't mind a walk."

They walked side by side, toward the far end of town. "You said last week that you're retiring again, which means you retired before. Correct?"

"Twice." The admission seemed to amuse him. "I can't seem to stay still, and I hoped coming here would make a difference. To the town, to the people. It's been on a downward trend for a while, losing folks to other places, towns with jobs. I kept thinking that if we could just start the ball rolling the other way, and gather momentum, we could catch the remaining pieces before it all falls apart."

"But it didn't work out that way," she observed, and he turned her way quickly, surprising her.

"But it did!" he exclaimed, smiling. "Not in the manner I expected, but then that's the way of things, isn't it? The good Lord sees beyond the bends in the road while we humans see the straight and narrow.

"So it's working fine, don't you think?" he asked her and when she looked surprised, he angled his chin toward her, then the town. "You're here. You've got other family heading this way. You got Heath to meet up with the other ranchers in town, now there's a solid group of stubborn men determined to go their own ways. And I haven't seen attendance at church or a memorial service like we had this weekend, so something's working, young lady. Something filled with faith and hope, and I think part of that is you. And Miss Corrie that came along with you. When I heard that Eric Carrington took some time away from his fancy horses and cattle to talk with regular folks, that was a big step in the right direction from where I'm standing. Oh, there's change brewing, Miss Lizzie Fitzgerald. And you're in the thick of it. Now if we can have folks learn to forgive and forget. To move on and not hold grudges." He swept the faltering town a long, slow look. "Well, that's my prayer right there."

They paused outside the square, worn rectory, the last building at the north end of town.

"For a long time folks in the Crossing have been going their own way, not sharing words or the Word. God's word, that is, about loving and caring and sacrifice and forgiving. But you and the boy, going house to house, inviting folks in, well…"

A winsome smile deepened the crinkles edging his eyes. "You got it started, and I'm only sorry I won't be here to see it all change, but that will take time and a man my age doesn't take time lightly." He winked, still smiling. "My daughter's due to pick me up tomorrow, but I'm glad I got a chance to thank you for that nice service today. And for being here. It makes me see how there is a season for everything, like the Good Book says. Your season is upon us."

He shook her hand, and for a quick moment, she didn't want to let go because the old fellow's wisdom struck a chord within her. Loving. Forgiving. God's word.

She'd never considered that her messages hadn't reached Heath. Messages always got through, eventually. Didn't they?

Reverend Sparks moved to the house, just as the church bells chimed the six o'clock hour.

The last toll trailed off softly. A zephyr breeze lifted upper leaves in a rustling whisper. She breathed in clean air, with the bright blue sky above and beyond the rugged peaks of mountains.

Then she thought of that woman at Uncle Sean's service, so happy to get a bit of news, of how one small flyer had brought neighbors and friends together.

A town worth fighting for.

She turned Honey's Money around and re-mounted, studying the layout of the mostly empty buildings as she went by. As she scanned them, the potential opportunity gleamed beneath shoddy exteriors. Shepherd's Crossing was a chance to start fresh, and make a difference in another way she knew well: a paper. Simple, to-the-point good reporting to reconnect the small town to its near neighbors.

But first, there was a mother dog who needed love and attention and Lizzie was determined she'd get it. By the time she got the horse settled, light was fading, but the two-story ranch home glowed from within. And inside, Betsy was presenting the world with tiny reddish gold puppies, and Lizzie sat right there, alongside the whelping box Cookie had brought in from the barn, and softly cheered her on.

Chapter Sixteen

Zeke's overnight stay at St. Alphonso's gave Heath plenty of time to think. And then berate himself. And then think again. And in between all that thinking, he did some first-class praying, the way he had when he was a kid.

How had this happened? How had everything gone so completely astray twelve years ago? Lizzie had spent all that time thinking he didn't care enough to come to her. To help her. To be with her.

He'd have done anything to help her. Then. And now. She must think him to be the worst loser to ever walk the planet, and yet—

She didn't. She'd come to the ranch calm and gentle. Ready to move on. He'd been the angry one, the defensive jerk, and all because he believed the lies he'd been fed like a stray dog grabs morsels of food.

Shame bit deep. Real deep. And the doctor had been correct, the chair he'd bunked in overnight was about the least comfortable piece of furniture known to man. But today was a new day. His boy was recovering. And Lizzie…well. One way or another he was going to convince her to give him a chance. To give *them* a chance.

"Your little fellow's going to be just fine," the doctor told Heath when she came into the cubicle to discharge them. "I've written down the name of that orthopedist in McCall. He'll set the wrist and cast it, and by midsummer Zeke will be right as rain. Everything was fixable, and that's a good thing."

Relief flowed through Heath as she handed him the discharge papers. He only wished his history with Lizzie could be mended that easily.

Zeke wasn't in the best of moods. When Heath had to help him with his seat belt latch because the boy's left hand couldn't maneuver the buckle, Zeke's lower lip stuck out. "I wish I never climbed that stupid old tree. It was a dumb thing to do and I'm never, ever, ever going to climb a tree again."

Heath saw the choice before him, plain as day.

He could agree with the kid and offer his son a measure of safety...

Or he could let Zeke grow up, encouraged to explore the world around him.

He chose the latter and kept his voice easy. "Hey, cowboy, climbing the tree wasn't the problem."

"It wasn't?" Zeke peered up at him, perplexed.

"Nope." Heath slid into the front seat and smiled at his boy through the rearview mirror. "Letting go was the problem. Next time you climb the tree, hang on tighter, okay? I climbed a lot of trees in my time, and it's a good thing for a cowboy to know. In case you get chased by a cougar or something."

The likelihood of that was about zero, but Zeke's brows shot up. "So it's really good to know how to climb a tree?"

"On my honor." He pulled onto the road and considered his words as he drove north.

He hadn't been honorable with Lizzie.

He'd let things go too far, then he'd left. Sure, they'd tossed him out, but what if he'd stayed and fought for the right to be with her? What kind of difference could that have made?

Eric Carrington had told the rest of the

major landowners that he thought their efforts to revitalize the town were too little, too late. He'd made his view clear at that quick meeting the previous day, and Eric could be right.

But did the same thing apply here? Could he make things up to Lizzie or was it too little, too late? The thought of her losing that baby all alone—

His throat choked and his gut clenched tight when he considered the years he'd spent believing the worst. What kind of a man did that?

He'd be the right kind of man this time. The kind she'd deserved all along.

He pulled into the driveway and parked the car. Corrie bustled out of the house. Relief brightened her dark features and a wide smile echoed his relief that Zeke was going to be all right. "There's our boy! And doesn't Cookie have all of your favorite foods waiting inside because we're that excited to have you back! How are you doing?" She bent low to ask the question as Jace and Ben hurried their way.

But no Lizzie.

"My arm hurts." Zeke climbed out of the car and leaned against Heath's leg. He sounded tired. He looked tired, too. "And my head hurts. But not as much as yesterday," he added. Then his profile brightened as he pointed inside. "Did Betsy have her puppies?" he asked. "That's all I kept dreaming about in the hospital, a chance to see little puppies. Are they so very tiny?"

"Come see."

Zeke swung about when he heard Lizzie's voice and his face lit up when he saw her holding the back door open. "My Lizzie!"

Zeke raced her way, even though he'd been told no running for at least a few days. Obviously that didn't count where Lizzie was concerned.

He threw his good arm around her. She cuddled him as if he was her own, and Heath's heart thudded all over again. She'd never had the chance to hold their baby. Nurse him. Sing to him. Rock him. She'd never had a moment of that sweet time while he'd had the pleasure of Zeke by his side for years.

How bitter that must have seemed when she first arrived. And yet she'd shown nothing but kindness and caring to his son.

"You have to be quiet." She put a finger to her lips as Heath moved their way. "Betsy is tired, but she's being a very good mom and good moms like their babies looked after. So no loud noises, okay?"

"Okay." He whispered the word, but then

pumped Lizzie's hand with his good one, clearly excited. "I can't wait to see them!"

They crossed into the laundry room. Betsy was stretched out on a thick, old blanket with a row of puppies nuzzling along her side.

"They are so very itsy-bitsy!" Zeke's voice started loud, then he reduced it, remembering. "I mean like the tiniest ever," he whispered, as if shocked. "Lambs aren't tiny like this."

"Much bigger," Heath agreed. He palmed his son's head. "All animals are different."

"They're so cute, but how come none of them have curly hair like Betsy?" Zeke asked as he squatted low. He began to look up and couldn't hide a slight wince.

Lizzie had squatted down alongside him. She saw the wince and smoothed a soft hand across his brow. "The curls will come," Lizzie assured him. "As they get bigger. You can have more puppy time later," she went on gently. "Go rest, and make Cookie feel good by sampling all the stuff he made just for you."

The big cook came up behind them just then. "Hey, little man. Welcome home." And when he gathered Zeke into his big, beefy arms, Heath realized something anew. Sean had built a community here on the ranch. People who cared and looked out for one another.

Now they needed to do the same for the town. But he didn't want to face that task alone. He wanted—

Lizzie smiled as Cookie carried Zeke into the kitchen to tempt the boy with culinary delights. Then she turned, realized Heath was looking at her, and the smile faded.

What could he say to bring the smile back? To bridge a gap that stretched so wide?

Wishing he'd practiced the words on the long drive home, he stayed in the doorway. "The puppies are doing okay? They look really good, Liz."

Chin down, she stroked Betsy with one hand. "These four seem fine. There was one that didn't make it. So sweet. So perfect. But she never took a breath."

He'd lost pups from the farm dogs before. Lambs, too. And each time he felt like he'd failed them somehow. "Liz—"

Regret drew her mouth down. She released a softly drawn breath as she continued to comfort the dog. "I buried her beneath the roses. I thought it would be a good spot."

"A real good spot." He ventured forward, unsure what to say, but knowing he had to say something, to open the conversation about their tiny son somehow. He drew closer, close enough to see the light shimmering along strands of her pretty hair. Close enough that a hint of vanilla and spice came his way. And then he restarted the conversation the only way he knew how, with an apology that came way too late, but was necessary, nonetheless. "I'm sorry, Liz." He paused and took a breath around the lump in his throat. "I'm sorry we lost him. And I'm sorry I wasn't there for you when you needed me. So sorry."

He didn't say "her," like he would have if he was talking about the puppy.

He was talking about their son.

"I never got your messages," he went on. "That old phone of mine broke on the way north and I didn't bother replacing it for a few months. And they tried to load all my old stuff onto the new phone, but coverage up here wasn't all that great back then. Neither were the phones. It's no excuse, I know, but I don't want you to think I'd have ever ignored you. I'd have come, Lizzie. If I'd known. I'm just real sorry it all came down that way."

She took a deep breath and faced him, at long last ready to talk. "I am, too. My heart broke that day because there was absolutely nothing I could do, Heath. And I'd have done anything to save him."

A tear trickled down her left cheek. Then her right one. He reached out and caught the tears with his hand in a touch so sweet and gentle it made her want to cry more. Not less. But the time for tears was over. She took a deep breath and said what she needed to say. "I'm sorry it got all messed up. Sorry about all the lies and secrets. I hate that kind of thing. I think that's why I jumped at this opportunity so quickly. To get out of the offices and into a barn. Horses don't lie. They don't cheat. They don't steal. To run an operation like we've got here is such a total blessing after being surrounded by my father's crimes. So Uncle Sean's timing was perfect. In so many ways."

She'd tipped her gaze down to the dog, but now she locked eyes with Heath.

He moved closer to her. So close she could smell the remnants of hospital soap on his hands and sweet creamed coffee on his breath. "I want to make a home here, Heath. On this ranch. In this town. Maybe I'll buy one of those little bungalows in town and fix it up, sweet and simple. And I can be the eccentric spinster lady who writes a little paper once a week. Just enough to bring folks together."

"I like the staying part." He sat down next to her as Betsy cared for her four busy babies. "But not the house in town."

"No?" She turned and met his gaze, and he was pretty sure her eyes twinkled into his. "Do you have a better idea, cowboy?"

He raised one hand up to caress her hair, her neck, her cheek. "I believe I do. And it involves a ring and a promise and a little boy who loves you already. But not nearly as much as I do, Liz." He took her mouth and kissed her lightly, then not so lightly. When he finally drew back, he left his forehead touching hers. "It's about us. And that's how I want it to stay. If you'll give me another chance, that is. I'd like to have the chance to court you properly."

"And quickly?" she wondered, smiling.

He laughed and kissed her again. "Quick works for me."

He pulled her into his arms for an awkward but beautiful hug, a hug she'd been missing for so long. Too long. "It sounds perfect to me, Liz."

She met his smile with one of her own,

then leaned her head against his broad, strong shoulder as the sated puppies dozed off, one by one. "It certainly does."

Epilogue

Lizzie finished tacking tiny twinkle lights around the second front window while Heath and Zeke hung a festive ornament in each pane.

"I've never seen anything so pretty in all my life, my Lizzie!" Zeke started to launch himself into her lap, but Heath caught him.

"Gentle with Mom, remember? There's a baby growing inside her."

"And it's so tiny right now," Zeke acknowledged because they'd been talking about this for weeks. "But in the spring it will be big enough to get born and be my brother or sister!"

"Which is exactly why we're all gathering out here tonight," announced Lizzie as the rest of the family and friends began to gather in the great room. "Zeke is going to tell us if this baby's a boy or a girl by eating a cupcake. If the filling is pink, then the baby's a girl. If it's blue…"

"Then it's a brother!" Zeke ran in a circle, because that was the kind of thing brothers did. And when the entire family and a host of friends had gathered with glasses of punch to toast the newest Caufield, Zeke took a bite of the cupcake.

He stared at it, then held it up for everyone to see. "I'm gonna have a sister, just like Jo-Jo!"

"A girl!"

"Oh, Lizzie." Corrie didn't wait for others to have a turn. She grabbed Lizzie into a hug and held on tight. "I am so happy for you, my precious girl."

"I know." Lizzie hugged her back as Heath tucked an arm around her waist.

"We've got something else to say," he announced as Charlotte and Melonie drew closer to Lizzie.

"We've picked out a name for our little girl."

Everyone got quiet.

"We're naming her to honor the person who has stood by us, all of us—" Lizzie indicated Mel and Charlotte "—all our lives.

In about four months you're all going to meet Coralee Caufield."

"You are naming that baby for me?" Corrie's eyes grew wide, then filled with tears. "You don't have to do that, you know. It's a fine name for an old Southern woman like myself, but—"

"It is the perfect name," Lizzie told her. "Stop fussing and be blessed. We couldn't name our little one after anyone better, and if she turns out to be a strong, gracious, faithful woman like her Grandma Corrie, then we'll be the happiest parents ever."

Tears slipped down Corrie's cheeks. Then Lizzie's. But before Charlotte and Mel could join in, Corrie stepped back. "Well, now, this is not the time for tears, Fitzgeralds! This is a time to celebrate so much good this past year." She reached back and lifted her little cup of punch and raised it high. "To new life. New chances. And to a baby, born in a manger, in a land unknown, I say Alleluia!"

A chorus of Alleluias rang out around them, and when Heath was finally able to grab a quiet moment with Lizzie, nearly two hours had passed. He put his arms around her from behind and laid his hands over their growing child. "Happy, Mrs. Caufield?"

"The happiest."

He kissed her cheek, then offered a sweet kiss to her mouth. "Thank you for making this the best Christmas ever."

She'd come to Idaho wanting to make the best of things, but never expecting to *have* the best of things.

But God knew. Through the winding and changing and uprising, he knew.

She leaned back against him, happier than she'd ever dreamed possible, then tipped her face up for his kiss, a kiss she wanted to enjoy forever as tiny lights twinkled around them. "The first of many, my love."

* * * * *

If you loved this book,
check out more heartwarming stories
from author Ruth Logan Herne

AN UNEXPECTED GROOM
HER UNEXPECTED FAMILY
THEIR SURPRISE DADDY
THE LAWMAN'S YULETIDE BABY
HER SECRET DAUGHTER

Available now from Love Inspired!

Find more great reads at
www.LoveInspired.com

Dear Reader,

I loved writing this story. I loved writing it because it gave me a chance to explore the two sides of forgiveness, and how our choices combine with our faith to make or break our paths in this world. Lizzie went through a tragic time at the age of eighteen. She should have had the best of everything by society's standards, and yet it all came crumbling down around her and she took the challenge and lived her faith. Moving on. Moving forward. Forgiving even though she could never forget.

But Heath carried his anger like a hankie in a back pocket. He believed without question and let anger eat at him for years.

Grudges are dreadful things. There are a lot of grudge holders in my family. I guess there are grudge holders in lots of families, but what a sadness that is, to be angry and then stay angry…for how long? Too long.

Forgiveness isn't just a Biblical reminder. It's sound advice. It's the basis for so much good in the world. That doesn't make it easy, I know…but it makes it worthwhile. A true heart is a forgiving heart.

I hope you loved this story! Thank you for

reading it, and you know I love to hear from readers, so feel free to email me at logan-herne@gmail.com or friend me on Facebook where I love to play and pray with readers, family and friends. And if you're wondering what's happening, visit my website ruthloganherne.com or follow me @RuthLogan-Herne on Twitter.

May you and yours be blessed in every way possible!
Ruthy

Get 4 FREE REWARDS!

We'll send you 2 FREE Books plus 2 FREE Mystery Gifts.

Love Inspired® Suspense books feature Christian characters facing challenges to their faith... and lives.

FREE Value Over **$20**

Get 4 FREE REWARDS!

We'll send you 2 FREE Books
<u>plus</u> 2 FREE Mystery Gifts.

Harlequin® Heartwarming™ Larger-Print books feature traditional values of home, family, community and most of all—love.

FREE
Value Over
$20

YES! Please send me 2 FREE Harlequin® Heartwarming™ Larger-Print novels and my 2 FREE mystery gifts (gifts worth about $10 retail). After receiving them, if I don't wish to receive any more books, I can return the shipping statement marked "cancel." If I don't cancel, I will receive 4 brand-new larger-print novels every month and be billed just $5.49 per book in the U.S. or $6.24 per book in Canada. That's a savings of at least 19% off the cover price. It's quite a bargain! Shipping and handling is just 50¢ per book in the U.S. and 75¢ per book in Canada*. I understand that accepting the 2 free books and gifts places me under no obligation to buy anything. I can always return a shipment and cancel at any time. The free books and gifts are mine to keep no matter what I decide.

161/361 IDN GMY3

Name (please print)

Address   Apt. #

City   State/Province   Zip/Postal Code

Mail to the **Reader Service:**
IN U.S.A.: P.O. Box 1341, Buffalo, NY 14240-8531
IN CANADA: P.O. Box 603, Fort Erie, Ontario L2A 5X3

Want to try two free books from another series? Call 1-800-873-8635 or visit www.ReaderService.com.

HW18

HOME on the RANCH

YES! Please send me the **Home on the Ranch Collection** in Larger Print. This collection begins with 3 FREE books and 2 FREE gifts in the first shipment. Along with my 3 free books, I'll also get the next 4 books from the Home on the Ranch Collection, in LARGER PRINT, which I may either return and owe nothing, or keep for the low price of $5.24 U.S./ $5.89 CDN each plus $2.99 for shipping and handling per shipment*. If I decide to continue, about once a month for 8 months I will get 6 or 7 more books, but will only need to pay for 4. That means 2 or 3 books in every shipment will be FREE! If I decide to keep the entire collection, I'll have paid for only 32 books because 19 books are FREE! I understand that accepting the 3 free books and gifts places me under no obligation to buy anything. I can always return a shipment and cancel at any time. My free books and gifts are mine to keep no matter what I decide.

268 HCN 3760 468 HCN 3760

Name	(PLEASE PRINT)	
Address		Apt. #
City	State/Prov.	Zip/Postal Code

Signature (if under 18, a parent or guardian must sign)

Mail to the **Reader Service:**
IN U.S.A.: P.O. Box 1341, Buffalo, New York 14240-8531
IN CANADA: P.O. Box 603, Fort Erie, Ontario L2A 5X3

* Terms and prices subject to change without notice. Prices do not include applicable taxes. Sales tax applicable in NY. Canadian residents will be charged applicable taxes. This offer is limited to one order per household. All orders subject to approval. Credit or debit balances in a customer's account(s) may be offset by any other outstanding balance owed by or to the customer. Please allow 3 to 4 weeks for delivery. Offer available while quantities last. Offer not available to Quebec residents.

Your Privacy—The Reader Service is committed to protecting your privacy. Our Privacy Policy is available online at www.ReaderService.com or upon request from the Reader Service.

We make a portion of our mailing list available to reputable third parties that offer products we believe may interest you. If you prefer that we not exchange your name with third parties, or if you wish to clarify or modify your communication preferences, please visit us at www.ReaderService.com/consumerschoice or write to us at Reader Service Preference Service, P.O. Box 9062, Buffalo, NY. 14240-9062. Include your complete name and address.